JOE AND THE UFO:
An American Folktale
A Novel
By
Daniel Sanchez—Leonetti

INTRODUCTION

BY

ROBERT "DOC" LEONETTI

JOE AND THE UFO: AN AMERICAN FOLKTALE

Joe And The UFO is a delightful novel that is full of heart. It's a story about hope, love, and rage and about greed, envy, power, debauchery, intrigue, humor and raconteurs. It is a depiction of an enervating Hispanic culture thriving to this very day in the towns and pristine mountains of the American Southwest. The fictional San Miguel Valley in Colorado could be any of these places and is a microcosm of what is right and wrong in contemporary America.

The story focuses on a financially troubled Joe Lucky who owns a small ranch that is about to be lost to foreclosure. The San Miguel Valley is the UFO Sighting Capital of the World. A flying saucer crashes in the meadow of Joe's ranch. Joe drags the UFO into his barn with his trusty old tractor to launch a proverbial wild and wacky World War III. He ultimately decides that the alien creatures incarcerated in the flying saucer are good and he must protect them despite his own financial loss. Joe is basically a good man, and like all good husbands and fathers, his primary motivation is to provide for his family. And, so it seems, initially there is no one there in the congregation of folks from his small rural community to provide support in his endeavors, only to castigate him. The consequences of his choice to save the space aliens hunkered in the UFO result in a maelstrom, a major social catastrophe.

When the United States government discovers that an unidentified object was taken to a secure place in his barn, the whole scenario morphs into a quagmire of intrigue, belligerence, manipulations laughable misrepresentations and comic incompetence on the part of the CIA and the United States military. He turns down a million dollar offer from the CIA because he knows whatever is inside the UFO will be removed and dissected like frogs in a government lab. Joe, like all of us, must search for answers to the childlike universal questions.

Who am I? From where did I come? What is good and what is real evil? What must I do about good or evil? And is there anybody else out there in this vast universe? But Joe is undaunted. He can see the people are barely getting along. Times are bad. The country is morally dead. Joe undertakes a physical and spiritual journey, and the only sure thing is that he will be changed by it. Facing bombs and assassins and defying danger and death to himself and those most dear to him, he marches on, brandishing a vessel of values only he can understand. And in the end, those values are also about a higher being.

Leonetti is a master of insights, a highly sagacious writer that gets to the essence of life's customs, values, mores, and ethics ensconced in American culture today. Here is a novel rich with archetypes, the characters that occur in the dreams and visions of all people and the deep myths of all cultures. The repeating characters of world myth such as the downtrodden hero, the gentle giant, the shape shifting La Llorona and the shadowy antagonist are why myth and other stories constructed on the mythological stage have the ring of truth. The characters are recognizable, a facsimile of all that we observe in our daily encounters with society. There are important lessons to be learned in reading this novel.

Joe and the UFO is unequivocally one of the best first novels, ranking right up there with Steinbeck's "paisanos" of *Tortilla Flat* or John Nichols' *The Milagro Beanfield War*. The story is a masterful representation of right and wrong, the need to love and believe, and, certainly, the ability to laugh at our foibles and shortcomings.

Robert "Doc" Leonetti
Trinidad, Colorado

IN LOVING MEMORY OF

CAROLYN JANET HOOK

MY DELOVELY

"In spite of everything I still believe that people are really good at heart."
DIARY OF ANNE FRANK.

CHAPTER ONE

A
SICKLE
moon hung in
the turquoise sky, like
a clipping from God's fingernail.
A thousand stars winked down on the slumbering
San Miguel Valley where the Texas doves cooed from the rocky nooks of Panocha Ridge. The ridge was a steep, rocky hill with a prominent forehead and a crew-cut top. Many seeds for valley children had been conceived on top of Panocha Ridge in the back seats of Chevies, Fords and even a few John Deere tractors.

The Texas doves, invaders from the south, were as amorous as the natives, multiplying in the biblical sense, but having, as Padre Gomez once said, more morals than his Sunday flock in church since they picked a mate for life. Texas was always the big brother to Colorado. Texas was bigger in land, money, hats and ego.

And the native Colorado turtledove, whose tiny pink breasts were usually tossed into succulent red chili sauces for Polenta dishes in the valley, were shy of their new kin who sported big plump breasts and cooed lavish and lusty songs. The impressive songsters also wore plumes on top of their heads, like ancient Roman helmets.

But the most troubling attribute of the Texas dove was a set of powerful lungs, which the people admired in the early stages of the migration. The citizens of San Miguel were inspired to see these big birds on the tree tops in the dusk of the evening until the "little cabrones" started to arouse the citizens out of their warm beds at 5 a.m. with incessant love songs. And when they didn't fly back South for the winter, like reasonable birds, Pachuco Pacheco blasted two of the crooners into the happy hunting grounds with a double-barrel Remington shotgun. And like any persecuted refugees in a new land, the Texas doves made a beeline for the heights of safety on the rocky Panocha Ridge.

So it was no strange thing when a Texas dove alighted onto the hood of Jerry Agee's pickup truck parked on top of Panocha Ridge and cooed for his mate in the cliffs below.

Jerry Agee lifted his big head out of Sarah Ortega's bosom, the daughter of the local Sheriff, and noticed the bird on the hood. He pounded his hand on the horn and tooted to no avail. The Texas Dove was perched as solid as the Chevy hood ornament. Jerry went back to the heaving bosom.

"Let's do it," he said in a husky voice. "I love you."

"I have no ring, hijo," said Sarah, "so get a clue."

"Please give me some panocha, honey," pleaded Jerry. "I love my Mexican candy!"

"Cochino," said Sarah. She was a dark, lovely girl with murky Spanish eyes and long black hair.

The pickup truck rocked from the wrestling match, and the Texas dove remained stubbornly on the hood. Suddenly the sky exploded into a dazzling show of mischievous lights, soaring and arcing across the Colorado heavens.

A pair of lights traveled a great distance, as if carried by wings, and then hovered directly over the pickup truck on Panocha Ridge. The lights slowly circled the truck in bright, pulsating bursts of red and orange. Jerry's head popped up like a puppet. He wiped the love fog off the rearview mirror.

"Is that your daddy?" he asked. "I see red lights flashin'."

His moon face was as pale as a pearl, and his flaming red hair matched his freckles. Sarah lay on the seat, brown and languid as a cat.

"Come here, my Howdy Doody," she said.

Inside the truck, the Hula girl in a grass skirt on the dashboard started to shake her hips. The radio clicked on, surfing channels until it stopped on the languid guitars of a Mexican love song.

"Turn off the radio," said Sarah.

"I didn't turn it on."

"Who did?"

He looked out the foggy windshield. The Texas dove was bathed in eerie light, one eye looking upward, head cocked and cooing incessantly. The bird attempted to take flight, but his wings froze in mid-air, and the dove was splattered against the windshield like a giant, bloody bug. A beak, tiny bones and feathers fluttered into the air. Jerry turned on the windshield wipers and managed to smear the bloody mess. Then the truck's engine mysteriously cranked to life and some unseen force gunned the engine. The truck slowly levitated up into the air, turned spookily in a full turn, and plunged back to earth in a thud of dust. Jerry's head hit the roof and he bit his tongue.

"Shit!" he said.

"Jerry?"

Jerry gunned the truck in his panic, but the gear was in neutral.

"Where is my sneaker?"

They exited the truck and Sarah hobbled over sharp stones to the edge of Panocha Ridge. They were blinded by the pulsating orange and blue lights of two flying saucers, resembling the planet of Saturn.

"They look just like the ones in comic books," he said. "Look at the rings."

Sarah's jaw seemed to drop to the ground. Below, in Joe Lucky's meadow, a milk cow grazed under the hovering, rotating flying saucers. The cow placidly munched on a mouthful of grass. The Texas Doves cooed from below. A dog barked, far away. Sarah babbled hysterically in Spanish. Joe Lucky's ranch house and giant red barn slumbered on the valley floor.

And then, in the wink of an eye, a laser fired a beam down from the belly of one flying saucer and sliced the cow in half-- head to tail--dumping brains, blood and entrails onto the grass.

One half of the cow's mouth still tried to masticate and one eye still blinked stupidly on the grass.

Sarah ripped out a lung-clearing scream. She pulled her hair and stomped her bare feet.

Jerry took hold of her flaying arms. "You're going to set the critters on us," he said. "Hush up."

One flying saucer made a screeching sound as if it was grinding gears and suddenly plunged down into the grass like an exhausted Frisbee.

Jerry and Sarah stood transfixed in moonlight and madness.

Joe Lucky lay in bed with his hands at his sides, stark naked. He was dark and fairly handsome at forty. He had black hair and brown piercing eyes. His nose was slightly crooked from an old football injury, but his smile was endearing and carried him through life as a likable chap. Nobody could stay mad at Joe Lucky for long, only the semi-mechanic Max Campos. He listened to his wife's soft snores beside him. She had one long naked leg exposed. Rachel was still a knock-out at thirty-eight. She had smooth pale skin, and a lot of grey brain mass between eyes that were as blue as the Sea of Cortez. She had a compassion for all creatures, man and beast. He often called her "Rachelicious" in moments of mischief and affection. He was sorry for all the stress he was putting on her and his little daughter Summer, a bundle of black-haired fury. And that was why he was awake, hands at his hips--all because he was buried in bank notes, bad luck, back taxes, empty bottles of Jack Daniels, and debt up to his naked buttocks. Sleep was as rare as money on the J. Lucky Ranch.

Thoughts of despair were galloping in his mind when he noticed the bright pulsating lights frolicking on his bedroom window. Joe Lucky tip-toed to the window. He extended his head directly into an eerie glow and he sucked in his breath.

Joe Lucky watched the flying saucer spin feebly in the grass of his meadow. The other flying saucer hovered in the air in bursts of red and orange, mourning its wounded mate. And then it soared off. . . taking giant frog leaps into space like a time machine until it dissipated into the winking stars. He ran for his jeans. He appeared on the porch, yanking on a scuffed cowboy boot but tripped and did a header into the dust of the yard. Duke, more black snout than anything, exited the dog house and barked up at the starry sky.

On Panocha Ridge, Jerry guided a near comatose Sarah to the truck. The vehicle's headlights were flashing on and off. The windshield wipers smeared the Texas dove into more red swirls. Jerry tossed the whimpering Sarah into the truck and in a moment they were speeding off the ridge, hell bent for sanctuary. Joe Lucky could see the headlights of Jerry's truck, zigzagging crazily down the switchback road.

He yanked on his other boot and ran for the huge red barn. Joe Lucky swung open the big double doors to reveal his ancient John Deere tractor. Tacked on the door of the barn was a hand painted sign:

COME SEE SNIPPY, FIRST HORSE
KILLED BY ALIEN CREATURES.
ADMISSION: ONE
DOLLAR.

CHAPTER TWO

"OF ALL THE places in the world," said General Snoopy Taylor. "Why did those alien bastards have to take a nose dive in the San Miguel Valley?" A young officer, Captain Jack Holloway, waited in Taylor's sleeping quarters on base. His face was flushed red by his scamper from the secret Norad Air Command Comcenter, deep inside Cheyenne Mountain near Colorado Springs, to the general's opulent quarters. Snoopy Taylor snapped on his blue jacket with four glistening stars. He was a crusty old bastard who flew over 50 missions during the illegal bombing campaigns in Laos and Cambodia during the Vietnam Conflict. Shot down in Cambodia, Snoopy Taylor evaded communist forces to walk out of the swamps by brute force with only a cut on his brow, a leech on his right nut and a bruise on his shin. More brawn than brains, more luck than fate, more lumbering than graceful, Snoopy Taylor was assigned to write the book on "escape and evasion" taught at Fort Benning, Georgia. He was a legend in the mind of the military.

"Are you sure about this, Jack?" he asked.

Captain Jack, fresh out of the nearby Air Force Academy, stood in awe of Snoopy Taylor. The General's oil portrait hung on the Academy dining room wall like a god, and cadets ate and spoke in hushed tones around it, as if the pigment of the paint sprouted real ears. Captain Jack fumbled for words:

"Yes sir," he said. "We tracked two of them. One is down. Condition unconfirmed. Do we need some boots on the ground?" Snoopy Taylor gazed into a mirror and he gently and carefully brushed his grey hair back. He patted a few stray hairs into place, and then slapped some cologne on his flabby cheeks. "Sound a Red Alert," said Snoopy Taylor. "Let's keep this contained from the media. I'll meet you down in the brain center."

CHAPTER THREE

THE SAN JUAN Mountains perched like saw's teeth in the dark sky. The little town of San Miguel huddled in their lap. East to west, furrowed fields ran for miles. Behind Julie One Owl's Cafe, an ancient apple orchard gave the valley an earthy, loamy smell. Main Street of San Miguel was only a paved block. The street began with a park of elm trees and green grass, and petered out with Emma's Convenience Store adjacent to Max Campos' dilapidated automobile and tire repair shop. Scruffy dogs curled up in front of old buildings and were too lazy to swat away mosquitoes with their long tails. There was no stop light. Main Street was a clean run of no traffic for the rare tourist who motored, mostly by accident, into this tranquility.

And this was a good thing because Jerry Agee's truck raced in from a reckless angle, horn tooting, and skidded to a stop in front of the tiny Sheriff's office. The wooden building was splashed with blue paint to try and make it look more gleeful. Jerry and Sarah ran barefoot into the office.

Sheriff John Ortega stretched out his five-foot-one inch frame in his squeaky chair, resting his legs and cowboy boots on top of a messy desk. A big Colt pistol hung on his hip. Jerry and Sarah stood in front of him, shaken to the bone.

"Mija, que pasa?"

"We saw a flying saucer crash in Joe Lucky's meadow! It cut up his cow, papa!" shrieked Sarah.

"Well, mija, tomorrow I'll go arrest it for cow murder."

"It's true, Sheriff Ortega," said Jerry. "It went down in Joe Lucky's meadow." "And where were you when you saw this flying saucer?" asked Ortega, squinting his eyes and plopping his cowboy hat on his bushy head.

"On the ridge, sir. Panocha Ridge!"

"You gringo scamp! I should arrest you

for molesting my daughter. Both
of you get in the truck. Show
me this flying saucer. And
there better be some
little green men
pissing in Mr.
Joe Lucky's
Meadow."

CHAPTER FOUR

JOE
LUCKY
puttered out of
the barn on his tractor.
Behind, he toted a four-wheel
trailer. He steered straight for the
meadow. Duke shot out of his dog house
and ran point for the smoking, groaning tractor. Snipes
exploded out of the grass and whistled straight for Panocha
Ridge. Crickets chirped from the dewy grass. He
bounced along, hooting and waving his baseball
cap as if he was at the end of a cattle
drive. "Star bright, starlight, make
my wish come true tonight," he
sang. The flying saucer
glistened like a new
dime in the
meadow.

CHAPTER FIVE

RED
LIGHTS
flashed. Sirens
reverberated. Black boots
pounded on the concrete floors.
Steel doors opened and clanged shut. Norad had come to life under the slumbering secret mountain, like soldier bees at the center of the hive. Snoopy Taylor looked at the bleeping dot on a wall-sized screen inside the comcenter. Communications specialists gazed into blue tracking screens.

NORAD had listening devices that penetrated deep into space. It was proudly said on many occasions by Snoopy Taylor that if a Russian took a crap inside the Kremlin, NORAD knew the exact grams of the dump. Snoopy Taylor sported a chestful of colorful ribbons. He tapped at the bleep on the monitor with his pointer stick.

"Is that the UFO, son?" he asked a communication specialist, who rose to his feet and stood trembling at parade rest. The general whacked him with his pointer stick.

"There is no room in my Air Force for an airman who is prone to wet his pants or wet the bed. Stand firm before an officer! Understood?"

"Yes sir," stammered the specialist.

He whacked him again for good measure.

"At ease, soldier," said the general.

The specialist relaxed. "It went down in sector 13, sir."

"Those San Miguel people are nut cases. They all have some bats flying around in their attics," Snoopy Taylor said. "Jack, scramble some fighters over that goddamn place."

Captain Jack picked up a phone and issued orders for the fighters at Peterson Air Force Base in Colorado Springs.

"Does the CIA know about this?" asked Snoopy Taylor.

"The spooks at Langley have their own spy in

the sky," Captain Jack said. "And they'll want a piece of the action." Snoopy Taylor paced nervously. "I'll probably lose a couple of stars over this damn mess," he lamented.

CHAPTER SIX

AT LANGLEY, Virginia, Bill LaPette exited CIA headquarters and boarded a black staff car. Roger Graham, private pilot for the CIA, sat in the back seat, puffing on a thick cigar. Graham studied the gruff, portly LaPette, who nervously drummed his fingers on his black briefcase. Graham knew this quiet agent could probably kill him with a prick of a pin.

The car rolled into motion.

"What's stirring in the wind this time CIA Bill?"

"Graham, you just fly the bird."

"Come on Bill, everything we know has a Top Secret clearance. We're lost souls. I like to know where I'm flying. Could be a hot zone and I might take a rocket up my tail."

"The San Miguel Valley in Colorado."

Graham puffed excessive smoke. "Never heard of it."

"Neither has most of the planet. There are a lot of chili eaters down there." CIA Bill looked pensively out the window, wondering why he got all the crap assignments. Jesus, he thought, I hope this doesn't take long. Mad hares and flying saucers. It sounded like a real dark fairy tale.

"Do they have a place to land or do I have to put my baby down in a beanfield?"

"There's a small airport. I want you to drop me off in the black of night and scoot out of there."

"Roger that," said Graham.

He looked at CIA Bill and thought him to be a true jackass. He had a geeky look to him, but under those horn-rimmed glasses was a dark side to CIA Bill. He never showed emotion which, Graham thought, put him in the sociopath category.

The staff car pulled up to a sleek jet. CIA Bill and Graham

walked briskly to the boarding stairs of the jet. "Well, buddy boy, throw in a pretty señorita for me and I'll hang around." CIA Bill had the patience of a snail. "I'm not going down there to put some meat in a taco," he said.

CHAPTER SEVEN

JOE
LUCKY
pointed a flash-
light on his dead cow.
One glassy eye looked up at him.
"Poor Toots," he lamented. "Summer is
going to cry some tears over this." Duke
slowly approached Toots and witnessed the carnage.
He turned his big snout toward the moon and howled in deep distress. And then Toots, perhaps in the final process of death, released a big burst of gas. The fart shook Duke to his wagging tail. He looked up at Joe Lucky and then took flight whimpering all the way across the meadow. Joe Lucky turned the flashlight toward the UFO, which spun a feeble half-turn in the grass. He looped cables over and under the UFO. Then he pulled a hook from his tractor winch. He hooked into the cables and slowly cranked the UFO onto his trailer.

"Welcome to earth, gentlemen," he said softly.

He pondered his circumstance on top of his tractor. He no longer seemed to fit in with this ancient and exhausted valley. He knew he would have to face the unknown. He also knew that he was at the beginning of a journey, and the only reward at the end of this journey could be his own demise. On the bright side, the journey would be one of change. He felt a great uneasiness stir inside his belly. But he exalted in this discovery. He faced a task worth getting out of bed in the morning, and he was ready to soar to the sun and melt his wax wings and reach enlightenment or bray in his free-fall to earth.

This was the critical point in his life. A crossroad of potential or doom. He was ready to break free from the mundane and enter into a new and wondrous world. All because a flying saucer had blown a fuse and crashed in his meadow. He felt he was chosen for something and he hoped the road ahead wasn't too bumpy.

The heavens turned into a chaotic display
of pulsating and arcing lights. Joe Lucky
cranked up his tractor and hauled
the UFO across the meadow
under the light of
the sickle
moon.

CHAPTER EIGHT

SHERIFF
ORTEGA PUT
the pedal to the medal
in his Ram Charger. It roared
past the potato fields and rows of
head lettuce and beyond the Japanese
Alligator Farm on desolate Highway 160.
The San Miguel Sheriff's Department, a one-man show, had dominion over the vast lands of chico covered plains and verdant green river valleys. Nestled high in the Colorado Rockies, the valley was cradled between the San Juan Mountains to the west and the beloved Sangre de Cristo mountains to the east. Mosca County was heavily populated with Spanish speaking people who had roots all the way back to the Conquistadors.

Sheriff Ortega was a busy man in Mosca County. Mosca was Spanish for fly — not the famous Spanish fly — but the horsefly that bit the hell out of Conquistador Don Diego de Vargas and his rag-tag army in the spring of 1690. The soldiers of fortune stumbled into the valley half dead from thirst. They camped at the great sand dunes. The sorry band of intruders were saved by the friendly "shining people" or Utes, who led Vargas by the hand over a towering sand dune, and pointed at the "fierce river of the north," or the Rio Grande in the distance. When Don Diego's thirst was quenched, he climbed another dune and stuck the flag of Spain into the hot sand. He promptly proclaimed the whole valley as territory of the king, and this included the friendly and smiling Utes whom he bound with ropes. He confiscated their elk stomachs filled with cool water and their buffalo meat. In his blackest moments, Sheriff Ortega said no peace had come to the valley since that puto Don Diego de Vargas stuck his flag into the very soul of the valley.

Ortega and his two charges accelerated down a dirt road through the entrance gate to the "J. Lucky Ranch." The house was dark. Ortega could see lights in the big red barn. He parked in front of the barn.

"I guess Joe is working late," he said. "Show me just where you saw this flying saucer that murders cows."

They walked off toward the meadow following Ortega's flashlight beam. And indeed Sheriff Ortega located the dead cow.

"Holy shit!" he said. "All I need is more cattle mutilations to stir up things." He poked a stick into the intestines and produced a fist-sized kidney on the end of the stick. Sarah started to gag. Jerry whacked his hip with his baseball cap.

"Dang, I told you, Sheriff."

"Yes, you did. But I don't see any little green men riding in a giant hubcap."

"It was here!" Jerry insisted.

"It's too dark to determine anything," Ortega said. "Let's talk to Joe."

They followed the frantic flashlight beam back toward the barn. Sheriff Ortega reached into the truck and tooted the horn until Joe Lucky emerged from the double doors, looking like a huge grasshopper with his welding goggles.

"Buenas dias," said Ortega. "I see you're burning the midnight oil."

"Sheriff, what you doing here so late?"

"The kids tell me that they watched a flying saucer fall out of the sky and crash in your meadow."

"The hell you say!" pretended Joe Lucky. "Did they see any spacemen?"

"No, but we found a dead cow."

"Must be Toots. She is the last of the Mohicans on this ranch. Toots must have eaten a bad dose of grass."

"Maybe. But the cow is opened up like the legs of that puta Martha Zuniga."

There was a loud noise in the sky. Everybody looked up. A pair of low flying fighter jets, dark and slick as bullets, roared over the barn.

"Pinche gabacho," Ortega said, "now the army is riled up."

"That's not the army," offered Joe Lucky. "That's the Air Force from Peterson Air Force Base. Those boys in blue are always chasing lights across this valley."

"No matter. I'm sure the army will come too, if these kids are right. You know how the people in this valley think of authority."

"Not too good, amigo," Joe Lucky said, "they elected you to four terms."

Ortega shuffled his feet, shifting his weight to the hip with the big Colt pistol. "So you gonna hang Toots up in the rafters like Snippy?"

"Now there's an idea. That might muster up some pesos."

"Joe, your mouth always worked too quickly for your brain. Can I have a look inside the barn?"

"Do you have a warrant?"

"No, pendejo."

The fighter jets zoomed back in the opposite direction. The barn suddenly glowed orange.

"When I went to bed last night," muttered Ortega, "I knew something bad was going to happen." Ortega made the Sign Of The Cross. "Get in the truck, children."

They boarded the truck. Ortega aimed a spotlight into the darkness looking for something amiss in the night. He aimed the spotlight on the doghouse. Duke offered a half-hearted bark. The truck did a doughnut in the yard and headed back for Highway 160.

Joe entered the barn. The shiny UFO reposed on the trailer. The barn was spacious with swallow nests high in the rafters. From one rafter Snippy, the complete skeleton of a female horse, was suspended in midair and held together by glue and wires. Above the elongated head of Snippy was a sign:

BORN OCT. 12 1964. KILLED BY ALIENS ON SEPT. 7, 1967.

Joe Lucky put Snippy up for sale on E-Bay but the largest bid was seven dollars and fifty cents. He paid eight dollars himself to keep Snippy. She had achieved reasonable fame as the first alien animal mutilation in the San Miguel valley. Someone or something had neatly clipped off her sexual organs. She was also eviscerated like Toots. Joe Lucky brought the dead horse home, boiled off the flesh and then wired together the bones and hung the skeleton in his barn. He charged one dollar a person for a personal viewing of the famous Snippy. Not many had an interest to see the famous horse.

    Joe Lucky supplemented his poor ranching skills as an artist. But like Vincent Van Gogh he never sold a piece. In every nook there were iron sculptures melted and shaped by his blow torch. Odd creations. The mayor of San Luis called them demented in a local newspaper story. They were fashioned from bits and pieces of scrap metal. Some had appendages and heads. Some were just torsos. Some were a tangled mess like horrific car accidents. Sculptures also hung in the rafters to give the barn the feel of a cave populated by gargoyles or giant bats. He had fashioned living quarters in one nook of the barn. There was a cot, a small refrigerator full of Bud Lite, and a microwave, a hot stove, a radio and a small television. The creaky barn was his artist's retreat. It was a place for quiet contemplation from all his money problems. Joe Lucky fired up his blow torch and climbed up a ladder onto the UFO. He adjusted the flame until it was a blue laser. He applied the flame onto the surface of the UFO. sparks gushed everywhere. They bounced like miniature
    Spheres off his eye goggles. He pulled off a glove and
      lay his hand on the strange machine. "What are
        you made of, spaceship? You're still as cold as
          a clam's heart." High up on the rafter, Snippy
           rattled her old bones and spun on the
            wires by some unseen magical
             breeze. Joe Lucky climbed
              down the ladder and sat
               on the cot. He looked
                at the flying saucer.
                 "You are a true
                   miracle!"

CHAPTER NINE

CIA
BILL PULLED
to the edge of Panocha
Ridge in a battered blue truck
with a C&H Plumbing logo on the dented
sides. He sported a cowboy hat with a turkey feather,
blue jeans and shirt. He wore scuffed sharkskin cowboy boots.
He stood on the ridge in the fading evening light and gazed through binoculars at the J. Lucky Ranch. He removed a text message machine from his pocket. Sophisticated and powerful, this newly developed gadget from the CIA lab was his favorite toy; other than the poisonous pin which he sported on the brim of his cowboy hat.

He pushed a button and neon lights blinked back at him. He typed: I have boots on the ground.

The machine blinked: Ten-four.

CIA Bill typed: The redneck rancher hauled the Cadillac from his meadow into his barn. I can see the trail in the grass.

The machine blinked: How did he do that?

He typed, annoyed: I don't know. Maybe he's Popeye and pulled it. Just confirm the mission.

The machine blinked again: Option One--steal the Cadillac. Option two--buy the Cadillac.

There was a pause.

Option three--kill the target and take the Cadillac.

CIA Bill typed: Ten-four from chilliville.

He clicked the machine shut and resumed gazing at the terrain through the binoculars. On his perch from a rock, shortly after sunrise, he watched Joe Lucky's battered truck ramble from the ranch yard and go down the dirt road to Highway 160. And from below, beneath his scuffed cowboy boots, he heard the Texas doves cooing from the nooks in the rocky walls.

Summer sat in Joe Lucky's lap and helped steer the truck. A fish I-pod swam on the dash, swaying its tail, like a real fish on dry land trying to get to water. Rachel looked beautiful in her spring dress with flower patterns. Joe Lucky stared at his wife. He was unlucky in money affairs but lucky in love.

The fish sang a ditty: "I'm happy to be me. I'm a happy fish in the sea."

"That fish talks too much," Joe Lucky said.

Summer tilted her head backwards and looked at her father. "I know. She wakes me up at night."

"We should take her to the sea and set her free," sang Joe Lucky.

"Daddy! You're silly."

"Yes, I am," he admitted, "from this day forth, you shall be known as Summer and the fish."

Rachel looked annoyingly at her husband. She clicked on the radio. A preacher spoke in a hushing voice. "We must ask questions in our own soul's journey to eternity. Who am I? Where did I come from? Where will I go when I die? What is good? What is evil? How do I choose between good and evil? Is there anybody else out there, my friend? Let us pray."

Rachel clicked off the radio.

"Where do we go when we die?" Summer asked.

"You'll go to heaven," answered Joe Lucky. "Because you're a good little girl and you have a magic fish."

"Why do we have to go to church?" she asked.

"Because," Joe Lucky interceded, resting his chin on the top of her head, "we are just taking up an insurance policy to get our darlin' girl to heaven."

"Can I take my fish?"

"Geeze daughter," Rachel said, "why so many questions."

"I guess fish are allowed in heaven," explained Joe Lucky. "Jesus fed a crowd with one fish. Or was it two fishes, honey?"

"I don't know," Rachel scoffed. "I wasn't there. Why don't you go ask Peter or Paul."

They turned onto Highway 160. Rachel pulled down dark glasses from the top of her head and gazed out the side window. Joe Lucky looked at his wife. He understood her dark mood swings. It was the stress of bills.

Rachel saw the acequias running full from the snow melt waters of the Rio Grande and Conejos Rivers. The ancient irrigation ditches were the life-giving arteries of the valley. The acequias were hacked out of the earth by hoe and shovel for 135 miles. They brought water to 62,000 acres of arid farmland. The people knew the value of water. They knew the value of the land. The land and water were inseparable. And without the acequias, tapping into the river to wet the fertile earth, everything would wither up and die on this high desert land.

And there was the sacred mountain. Debate about the mountain was like sucking cold air into a bad tooth. The people had hunted and fished on the mountain for nearly three centuries. They had passed down their Spanish land grants from generation to generation. They had gathered wood and rested in the mountain's wonderful nooks and dipped their aching feet into the cool springs. And then a rich and clever gringo pulled some strings and purchased the mountain. He put gates with locks on the old roads and the sacred mountain was pulled from under their feet. And the gente had lost their soul. And everyday, when the people of San Miguel stepped out of their simple dwellings, they looked reverently toward the mountain with aches in their broken hearts.

Rachel inhaled the clear desert air that came rushing off the mountain. She filled her lungs and felt them rejoice.

"Look, Rachelicious, the dandelion greens are up," proclaimed Joe Lucky.

Rachel noticed people in the meadows wearing colorful shirts and blouses with backs-bent to the earth. They were picking dandelions for salads and dipping knives into the grass to cut the leafy plant loose by severing the pale root. She might do some picking herself after church, she thought. Dandelion picking was a mind healing experience, not a task. It was a chance to get your hands dirty in the earth. Joe Lucky loved dandelion salad splashed with olive oil and vinegar. She tossed in white onion, bacon bits and sliced boiled eggs. It was one of the small joys in life.

And besides, Pete Barros made the best damn wine from

dandelions and Joe Lucky had sipped a few jugs of the wine in his time. The fish swam rhythmically on the dash.
    Joe Lucky and Summer steered the truck down the highway. "Daddy, will I be back in time to watch cartoons?" Summer asked.
"I think so," Joe Lucky said, "if Padre Gomez isn't feeling too much of the Holy Spirit."

CHAPTER TEN

SAN
MIGUEL
was the oldest
town in Colorado.
Spanish homesteaders, as
far back as the 1690's, had planted
pinto beans, the ever dependable maize
and the old apple orchard. The little hamlet
also boasted the oldest parish church in Colorado, but
the town wasn't incorporated until the Anglo immigrants came
pouring into the valley in 1851. The Japanese followed in the
early 1900's to take up the profitable tasks of planting potatoes.

There were many legends circling around the Virgin de Guadalupe Church, a wonderful adobe structure with a tower spiraling upward like a pared pencil, merging into a white wooden cross at the zenith. Most historians and the natives accepted the "broken wheel" legend.

Inspired by Don Diego, a group of Spanish settlers rambled along the Los Caminos Antiguos, the "Ancient Roads," and entered the valley in search of the loamy river lands. They drove goats and sheep in front of their weary oxen into the valley. The Virgin de Guadalupe was roped into one of the carts. The beautiful statue was cast in Madrid and sailed across the ocean to Mexico City and then was lassoed into the cart for the bumpy journey across the vastness of New Mexico. Deep in the valley, the cart's wheel finally petered out and snapped into pieces. The Virgin de Guadalupe toppled out the cart and miraculously landed on its base without a nick. The Spaniards fell to their knees and rejoiced in this milagro. This was the end of their journey. The Blessed Virgin had spoken. They cut down timber and proceeded to build their church directly over the statue. And so God was planted into the valley as firmly as the ancient apple orchards.

Joe Lucky blessed himself with holy water inside the old

church. Rachel and Summer made the Sign Of The Cross. They sat in a pine wood pew. Padre Gomez, stocky and short, looked more like a man of the fields than a Catholic priest. He stood before the neo-Gothic altar and the statue of the Virgin de Guadalupe. Santos and retablos and fresh fruit from the orchard decorated the platform for the Blessed Virgin. Colorful murals dressed the plaster walls, expressing the joy and pain of God and faith.

    A brass crucifix was in place on top of the altar. Padre Gomez recited mass. Three altar boys, dressed in white robes, followed in his steps as he rattled smoky and pungent clouds of incense. The church was filled with brown and white faces, some as young as tadpoles and some as wrinkled and old as the church. Joe Lucky sang loudly. Rachel had less religion in her song. Summer played with the fish on the bench pew. A solitary guitar player strummed chords with the notes of a piano as background. The congregation knew each song by memory, chanting in unison from prayer to song and merging effortlessly from English to Spanish. The little Virgin of Guadalupe church had a lot of lust for the Lord.

    On the corner of Main Street, next to Max Campos' Auto Repair shop, the wonderful smell of Julie One Owl's red and green chili sauces permeated the entire hamlet. The smoking green chili was made from the famous and fleshy mirasol from the chili fields of Pueblo, Colorado and came in levels of mild, hot, and "kiss the devil's ass" hot. The red version was stirred into a succulent creation from the powdered red chili from Chimayo, New Mexico, and it packed a heavyweight punch too. Julie One Owl bought the red powered chili from a traveling man. The smell of chili was so enticing that Max Campos came out and lifted his hawk nose to sniff the air. He wore greasy overalls. He scratched into his long ponytail of graying hair with a wrench. He watched Joe Lucky park his truck in front of the cafe.

    Summer ran into the cafe ahead of Rachel and Joe Lucky. They selected a table. The tables were covered in red and yellow oilcloth. Colorful sombreros hung on the wall with strings of dried red chili ristras. Near the entrance, an iron spiral staircase twirled upward to Julie One Owl's living quarters on the second floor. In the kitchen, Julie One Owl pulled off her apron and came into the dining room.

"Hola!" said Julie One Owl. She wore a two strand bone necklace. Her high cheekbones were the genetic result of her Lakota father, Rain In The Face, and her Spanish mother. She was dark and exotic and walked with a grace in her swaying hips. She had more curves than a mountain road. At each graceful turn the turquoise clicked on her wrists. She wore a T-shirt that showed Custer with an arrow through his broad-brimmed hat and beneath was a bemusing line:

"WHERE DID ALL THOSE DAMN INDIANS COME FROM"?

"Morning, Julie, what you got in the frying pan?" asked Joe Lucky.

Julie One Owl studied the Lucky clan. Joe Lucky and his cute daughter had dispositions like yellow flowers. Rachel, she thought, was a brooding purple poppy, but Joe Lucky's frivolous and goofy gambles with money had some influence on her personality. Joe Lucky had a lust for life, and that translated in the valley as a drinking problem. He put many dents into his ancient tractor because of Mr. Jack Daniels. Once, he knocked down a telephone pole with his tractor and the valley went silent for three days. Some men were born for money. Joe Lucky wasn't. Summer put her I-pod fish on the table and it quietly swam in place.

"I wish somebody would put a hook in it," joked Rachel.
"Hola, Summer, how are you, mija," asked Julie One Owl.
"Hola," said Summer.

Julie One Owl pulled out a wild blue Columbine from a vase and stuck it into Summer's black swirls of hair.

"I have red and green enchiladas. But if mija wants a hamburger I can have Thomas slap one on the grill."

"I want a hamburger and fries," Summer said.

"I'll take the enchiladas with green," Joe Lucky said.

"I'll have red," said Rachel.

"Mucho Gusto, said Julie One Owl. She walked off with turquoise rattling. Thomas Lopez, the cranky cook, was sleeping on a cot in the kitchen. His wrinkled face emitted such loud snores that they threatened to wake himself from his own blissful sleep. Julie One Owl roused him from his slumber.

'Que pasa?" he said, annoyed.

"I need a red and a green," ordered Julie One Owl.

In the dining room, Joe Lucky reached out and touched Rachel's face. "Honey, do you feel OK?"

"Sure, Joe, what you got in the barn?"

Joe Lucky gave her a sheepish look.

Max Campos entered the diner. He had removed the overalls and wore a green jungle shirt with the 101st Screaming Eagle Airborne patch, blue jeans and Nikes. He sat at the only stool by the cash register.

"Julie!" he yelled. "Bring me some of those enchiladas, smothered in green chili." He twirled on the stool to look at the Luckys. There was an icy gap between Joe Lucky and Max Campos. A negative karma. A mutual dislike. Joe Lucky's high school prank had festered in Max's heart longer than the Vietnam War. It was a prank, as Principal Zeke Pugnet reported to the school board, never done before in the annals of sports. During the homecoming football game with Mosca, Joe Lucky used a biology scalpel in a doggiepile at the 40-yard line to slice Max's football pants clean down the buttocks. On the next play, Max, a speedy halfback, dashed 40-yards for a touchdown with his buttocks fully exposed. Max stood in the middle of the endzone with arms lifted high in triumph as the San Miguel Stadium roared with laughter. Max never forgave his quarterback, the gringo jackass. Not even when Zeke Pugnet slapped Joe Lucky on the side of the head and demanded an apology in front of the whole school. Joe Lucky mumbled his apology with sincere shame on the tiny drama stage inside the gym. Max was christened with the nickname of "mucho hete," or much buttocks. It was a fine moniker for a woman but it had a stigma for a man of brass balls from the 101st Airborne.

"Hey, gabacho," said Max, "I heard you had an incident on your ranch last night."

"Hello Max," Joe Lucky said. "There was no incident. Can't you let dead dogs lie?"

Julie One Owl crashed through the swinging doors with three plates balanced on her right arm. She went to the table. Her enchiladas were the star of the little cafe, paired with pinto beans and Spanish rice and a side dish of hot tortillas. She placed the works of art on top of bright oilcloth on the table.

"You're a real Picasso," said Joe Lucky.

"Well you certainly ain't," said Julie One Owl. "When you going to sell one of those damn things hanging in your barn? Red for you. Green for you. And one of Julie's special burgers for mija and her mucho talking trucha. And you, Max, don't bother my customers, rare as they are." She walked toward Max and spun his stool around, and went back into the kitchen.

Summer attempted to feed her fish a French Fry. "Might have better luck with a worm," said Joe Lucky. "Daddy, I ain't got no worm." Despite herself, Rachel laughed. Joe Lucky and Rachel forked food into their mouths with gusto. "Pendejo," said Max, "something crashed at your ranch. I'll find out. Remember, cholo, Pinocchio's nose grew like a hard-on when he told a tiny, little white lie!"

CHAPTER ELEVEN

IN
SAN MIGUEL
Max walked point
for a vocal mob gathered
in front of Ortega's office. They
made threats with rusty handguns,
rakes and hoes. Max shouted, "Sheriff Ortega!
We need to talk!" Ortega came out of his office, hands
on hips. "Look at all the gente. Did Cinco de Mayo come
early?" asked Ortega. The mob uttered bad words in Spanish.
One voice roared, "they say Joe Lucky found a flying saucer on his ranch."

Ortega scratched into his whirls of white hair. "I went out there last night. I didn't have a close encounter."

Another voice came out of the mob: "Someone said he hid it."

"They say. Someone said. Go home." Ortega stood his ground as the mob pressed closer.

Max said, "that little gringo boy, the one who looks like Howdy Doody. You know, the boy doing your daughter, he said he saw it crash in Joe Lucky's meadow."

Ortega's face turned from brown to black. "Max Campos, you little shit! Callete tu boca! You should be watching the mailman and not my daughter. He's delivering more than the mail to your corazon Mabel Baca."

"You-son-of-a-bitch!" said Max.

Another voice emerged from the mob: "If Joe has a flying saucer, those pinche Army cabrones will come down here. We'll have anarchy."

"We have anarchy right here!" retorted Ortega.

Max hollered: "Some bullets are gonna fly, sure as a squirrel shits in a tree. And you, Ortega, might get one of those full metal jackets up your brown highway!"

Ortega took extreme offense. He removed his big Colt pistol

and fired six rapid rounds up into the air.
"What goes up must come down," Ortega calmly said.
Time stood still, or rather the mob. All eyes looked skyward.
Then the mob scrambled for pickup trucks across the street.
Some ran down the street. Others tossed encumbering hoes
and rakes. All ran with heads tilted skyward while
the whole procession was chased by barking
dogs. Ortega entered his office and
promptly put a sign in
the front window:
BACK IN 15
MENOS.

CHAPTER TWELVE

THE
ANARCHY
was inside the barn.
Joe Lucky stood on top
of the UFO ring and tapped
on the flying saucer with his hammer.
He put his right ear against the smooth cold
metal and listened for any response. The flying
saucer looked as dead as a seashell. He fired up his torch, yanked down his eye goggles and once again blasted sparks everywhere. The dawn peeped over the San Juan Mountains, like a bomb blast frozen in time. Coyote pups yelped from the meadow. Two Texas doves cooed in the giant oak tree by the ranch house, making love in the glistening green leaves. Rachel appeared on the porch in her robe. She walked across the yard with a breakfast tray of eggs, bacon, toast and a glass of orange juice. She called for Duke but heard only a whimper from inside the doghouse. She could smell the loamy earth, and the pungent chico bushes. She paused to take in the sounds and smells. This was home. It was an immense land with few people. She pulled open the heavy barn doors and stood with an open mouth.

"Damn you, Joe. Whatcha done now?"

Joe looked at his wife through his goggles. "You mean Snippy?"

"Nobody comes to see that damn horse anymore. I mean that thing there!"

Joe Lucky lifted his goggles. "I found her in the meadow. Sorry to say they cut up our milk cow. Some sort of experiment. Her titties were as dry as witches' tits anyway."

"Summer loved that cow, Joe."

"I know, honey. I'll tell her that Toots went up into the great milk barn in heaven." He climbed down from the flying saucer.

"And me, Joe. What are you going to tell me? We're losing the ranch, and you're monkeying around with. . .let the government have that thing!" She put the tray on the table near the cot.

"Honey, come look at this." Joe Lucky pulled down his goggles and applied the flame of his torch to the belly of the flying saucer. Sparks bounced off his goggles. He waved for Rachel. She approached apprehensively.

"It's not even hot," he said. "Put your hand on it."
Rachel touched the machine. "Sweet Jesus, Joe. Are there real spacemen in there?"

"Somebody had to drive it."

"Are they going to come out?"

"I think so, when they're ready."

"Get rid of it, Joe. We could have another Day the Earth Stood Still. Those things could murder us in our sleep! They murdered our milk cow, didn't they?"

"Honey, remember what the preacher said on the radio. What is good? What is evil? What we gonna choose? This is not heads or tails. I have to believe there is something good inside there. Some hope for this sick planet. We need some sort of affirmation, honey." He picked up a hammer and tapped on the shiny metal.

"They're not from here, Joe!"

"Of course not! Why do you have to be so cynical?"

"Cynical! The whole world is cynical. They killed King Kong didn't they? Worry about this damn ranch or we'll be homeless and dining from garbage cans."

Summer appeared at the door standing in the golden sunlight. She wore pink pajamas and rubbed her sleepy eyes. "Mommy, I'm hungry."

"Look there, Rachel, isn't that my happy feet?"

"Daddy, my name is Summer. Not happy feet." She pointed at the flying saucer, her eyes filled with childish wonder. What's that?"

"We have some guests," said Joe Lucky. He looked at her, his child in the sunlight, and his heart nearly burst with love for his daughter.

"Do they live in there, daddy?"

"Not exactly. It's a kind of car."

"It's silly looking. It has no tires."

"Good point," answered Joe Lucky. "Must be a time machine to travel from star to star."

Rachel scooped up Summer. "Let's go have breakfast, darling. Let's leave daddy with his mad schemes. I don't want you coming into the barn anymore. Okay?" "Why, mommy?"
"Never mind why." Rachel banged the barn doors
so hard that Snippy clattered up on the
rafter. Joe sat down to his breakfast, still sporting his thick
goggles, and gobbled
the yellow yolk
of a fried
egg.

CHAPTER THIRTEEN

DOWN INTERSTATE 25 from NORAD, the Fort Carson Army Base also elapsed into a secret flash mode. Green Jeeps and Hummers raced to and fro. Colonel Cal Smith rode in one of them. His Jeep stopped in front of the Long Range Reconnaissance Patrol Building. The LRRPS were famous and elite, small teams created on the premise of gathering intelligence rather than engaging the enemy. But when they did engage, let Betsy bar the barn door because they were meaner than a wounded Colorado badger. Colonel Cal crashed through the door to the cries of "Attention!" A seven-man team of LRRPS sprang to their feet, clicking polished black boots.

"At ease," said Colonel Cal. "Take your seats."

Colonel Cal sported a shaved bald head. He carried 250 pounds of brute force, and paced with his Patton pointer stick.

"We've a secret mission, boys," he said. "It seems we have a crashed UFO on a ranch in the San Miguel Valley. The Air Force, those sissy boys, aren't smart enough to get downwind of their own farts. I want the Army to save the day!"

A LRRP, young as a puppy, eagerly raised his hand. "Are we to engage the enemy if threatened, sir?"

"There's no enemy, son. Not yet. Point of contact is a man named Joe Lucky. Don't shoot him, even if he has a pitch fork up your ass. Engagement would be a terrible public relation disaster. The people in the valley know about this UFO. Soon the press will too. I'm sending in a small unit. I want you in foxholes. We're setting up a communication unit in the valley and this will be your home base. We don't want another Waco or Ruby Ridge. No black eyes this time, understood!"

"Yes Sir!" shouted a chorus of cries.

"Let's get our jump wings on the

ground and beat the Air Force
to the punch," said Colonel
Cal. "Go Army!"
roared the
men.

CHAPTER FOURTEEN

JOE
LUCKY
tooted the
tractor horn. "Hold
your horses," shouted Rachel
from the porch, wearing a sexy swimsuit
and holding a picnic basket. "Come on, Summer,
hurry up honey or daddy will get a hernia!" Summer appeared
on the porch in a swimsuit. She hoisted a big blue-eyed doll
nearly half her size and a deflated inner-tube.

Joe Lucky swung Summer and the doll up onto the tractor and placed her on the floor by the gear box. Rachel climbed aboard and sat facing him on the tractor seat. He passed the red barn looking to see that the heavy chains were still on the doors.

"All parties hang on!" yelled Joe Lucky. He shifted into gear and the tractor bounced into the meadow toward a distant windmill. They puttered along, shouting and laughing. The sky was robin-egg blue and streaked with white clouds like a porcelain bowl. The meadow was full of dandelion seeds that sailed off into the air like tiny parachutes. Some landed in Rachel's hair and Joe Lucky blew them free with his breath.

"I'm getting excited Joe," said Rachel, bouncing in front of him.

"I am too, honey."

"I know," she said. "I can feel you, dummy. I love this ranch, Joe. I'm sorry for being moody. I just worry about losing it."

"I know."

"And now. . .that thing in the barn."

Joe Lucky sagged in his tractor seat. He stomped on the squeaky brake and the tractor came to a stop at the towering windmill, which creaked wearily in the air. Gurgling water flowed out of a pipe and spilled into a tank on the ground. Rachel set up a blanket and picnic on the grass. Joe Lucky lifted Summer and the doll off the tractor. Summer set her big doll on the grass and stood looking at the tank. A few dragonflies buzzed on the surface of the water like tiny motor boats.

"Daddy, the bugs are drownin'."

"Well, honey, when you get into the swimming pool you can rescue them."

"That's not a swimming pool."

"Yes it is. It's a poor man's swimming pool."

"Cows drink out of that!"

"Summer, we don't have any cows," explained Rachel, blowing into the floating tube topped with a duck's head.

"I blame our cattle failure on Max Campos," said Joe Lucky. "The talk is that he put salt peter into this tank. And our bulls went flaccid."

"That's just town talk," scoffed Rachel. "I never heard of such a trick. Besides you dally in this tank and you seem fine to me in that department."

"Yeah, but I float in the water. I don't drink it."

"You should really try to get along with Max Campos."

"Toots," said Summer, "she drinks out of this tank."

"Toots went away to the big milk barn in the sky," said Joe Lucky.

"Toots is dead?" asked Summer. Tears came into her big brown eyes. She contemplated this dreadful news and made a sad face.

Joe Lucky picked her up and swung her around in a circle before depositing her inside the tank.

"Toots had a long life for a milk cow," Joe Lucky explained. "She's up in heaven and doesn't have to fret over giving milk anymore."

"She can just eat all she wants in the pastures of heaven," added Rachael, "and we should be very happy for Toots."

Rachel placed the floating tube over her head. Rachel and Joe Lucky climbed into the tank.

They giggled like children. They leaned up against the tank, and exchanged a long kiss. Rachel looked up into blue skies. Summer floated around the tank, propelled by her tiny splashing feet

and buoyed by her ducky tube. "I hope
nothing else falls out of the sky," said
Rachel. "Honey, I would like to
have another one," he said.
Rachel splashed water
into his face. "Isn't
one UFO enough
of a frigging
fret?"

CHAPTER FIFTEEN

SHERIFF
ORTEGA STOOD
on the edge of Panocha
Ridge. Below, he watched Joe
Lucky secure the barn doors with chains
and walk into the house. From a rocky outcrop,
CIA Bill studied Ortega. A Texas dove flew up from the cliff
and landed on Ortega's truck. The big bird tilted his
head and looked to the heavens with one eye. The
dove cooed up at LRRP's silently gliding down
on silk parachutes toward earth. Ortega
watched one parachute catch wind and
sail off course toward the north.
"Madre de Dios!" he said.
"The Army is here! I
wonder if I can
resign this
pinche
job?"

CHAPTER SIXTEEN

PACHUCO
WAS DREAMING
that he was in a bar in
Tijuana. Half-naked women
wiggled around him like earthworms.
He licked the back of his hand for salt and
fired down a dream shot of tequila, and grunted
in his sleep with deep satisfaction. Someone, he did not know
who, perhaps a jealous lover, came into the bar with a gun and
fired a shot at him. . . BANG!

Outside, the wayward LRRP crashed boots first into the flimsy tin roof of Pachuco Pacheco's chicken coop. The rooting chickens flew into a frenzy, beating their short wings and flying nowhere as feathers floated in the air. The white dust of chicken poop shot up through the gap in the roof. Inside the tiny adobe house, Pachuco searched for his bifocals. He was thin as a river reed in his white night gown. He placed the bifocals on his bony nose. His hair was thick and messy like old Moses on the mountain. At eighty years old, Pachuco had buried three wives and many lovers. None of them worth a centavo. He located his slippers and yanked his Remington shotgun from under the bed; (Sheriff Ortega let him keep it for the Texas doves and he did fire the first volley in the bird wars) and then turned on the lights in the kitchen. Muttering curses in Spanish, he went onto the sagging porch and stood peering into the darkness. His chickens were squawking like his first wife.

"Venga aqui, you chicken stealers!" shouted the old man. "Andale, cabrones!"

Pachuco pulled back one hammer on the breach and fired wildly into the night. Shotgun pellets ripped through his long johns that dangled on the clothes line. The LRRP paratrooper panicked at the sound of the blast. He exited from the madness inside the coop, and was entangled in his white parachute. His head appeared round from the shape of his helmet and only black jump boots appeared out of the shroud of white silky parachute.

Pachuco was horrified. He stood paralyzed with fear between the two small windows that glowed from the light in the kitchen. The paratrooper stumbled blindly in the yard. His arms and legs kicked violently to free himself. Pachuco let loose the second barrel but it sailed high into a tree. Leaves fluttered down into the yard.

"Un espiritu maligno!" shouted Pachuco. He hobbled off for his old Chevy truck and tossed in the shotgun. He climbed into the truck and sped off, honking the horn to ward off the evil spirit.

Back at the ranch, Duke stuck out his black snout from the dog house and sniffed the air. He looked up and watched the LRRP's float down to earth and thump in the far recesses of the meadow like fruit falling in the old orchard. He offered his half-hearted bark and receded back into his dog house. The LRRP patrol tossed down their heavy packs and started to cut slabs of grassy sod with pack shovels. Then they dug deep foxholes.

Joe Lucky stuck his head out the bedroom window.

"Hey Duke, hold down the fort, boy. Bite them bastards if you get a notion." Duke whimpered from inside his dog house.

"Joe, come to bed," said Rachel.

Pachuco stomped on the brake and skidded to a stop in front of the San Miguel Church. He ran into the sanctuary with his shotgun, trying to cock both horse-head hammers. He lay prone in front of the Virgin de Guadalupe.

"Blessed Virgin, please forgive my evil ways. I do not want to go to Tijuana."

Padre Gomez entered, wearing his own white night gown.

"Is that you, Pachuco? Why did you bring that gun into the church? Esta loco?"

Pachuco rose to his knees and genuflected to the Virgin de Guadalupe. He shivered with imaginary cold. "Padre Gomez don't take offense, but how else am I, a viejo, to do battle with a diablo. He's at my casa. Eating my dear chickens!"

"You will go to hell for lying, old man. And where are your clothes. This is disrespectful. What devil?"

"He looked like Casper."

"Casper the ghost?"

"Si, Padre. He looked like him. I know it! Pray for them, Padre."

"The only chicken I'll pray for," said the exasperated priest, "is one in Julie One Owl's frying pan." He lifted a crucifix and kissed it for more patience. He took up a book of matches and lit a candle. Pachuco lay on his back in front of the altar, his frail chest rising and falling in his fear.

"Forgive us, Holy Mother, but we have a misunderstanding in the middle of the night. And you have more important issues at hand." Padre Gomez turned to Pachuco. "If you don't take that gun out of here" he said sternly, "I will summon Sheriff Ortega." "Ortega is watching Joe Lucky's ranch. Renaldo Chavez saw him." "Then I will throw you in jail myself, viejo!" Padre Gomez sat in a pew, dejected.

CHAPTER SEVENTEEN

CIA
BILL CRAWLED
past the dog house with
a rope around his neck, a crowbar
in his belt and a flashlight in his hand.
He tossed a biscuit in front of the dog house.
Duke stuck out one big paw and fetched the biscuit.
CIA Bill continued to crawl toward the barn, swift as a lizard. He hurled the rope over the weather vane and climbed onto the roof. He yanked out squeaky nails with the crowbar, removed boards and descended into the barn by rope. He dangled in the darkness. He flicked on the flashlight and the beam zigzagged through the rafters.

CIA Bill saw the most horrendous figures, nightmares of the mind, hanging from the rafters like weird giant bats. Did Joe Lucky join the aliens to hatch these beasts on mankind? The flashlight beam darted over the entire output of Joe Lucky's hellish, artistic mind. CIA Bill gasped for breath. He cursed the CIA. He knew that someday he would suffer a ghastly death. He just didn't want to die in this lonely place. The CIA never claimed any agent's body. Agents had to be content to go to the grave with only the notion of being a great patriot.

Then he bumped into something in the dark.

There was a clattering noise.

CIA Bill nearly had a stroke when the light flashed onto the huge skull of Snippy and her mocking horse teeth. CIA Bill and Snippy were so close they could have French kissed. He screamed in terror.

"Son of a bitch!" said CIA Bill, and pulled himself up the rope as nifty as a monkey. The flashlight crashed down onto the flying saucer, which emitted a pitiful beam. Up in
the sky, Predator drones circled like buzzards over
the J. Lucky Ranch. CIA Bill repelled off
the barn and took frantic flight

from the yard, but he tripped
over a discarded sculpture.
He tumbled like a
circus bear
into the
night.

CHAPTER EIGHTEEN

AT
NORAD,
Snoopy Taylor
looked closely at a series
of photographs. A communication
specialist tinkered with the images, zooming
them into larger shapes. "I can't tell what's inside the
barn, sir," he explained. "But there are some strange holes in the meadow."

"Make a guess on the holes," demanded Snoopy Taylor.

The specialist zoomed a photograph to fill the huge screen. He saw a roll of toilet paper on the grass. "If I had to guess, I would say some sort of foxholes."

Snoopy Taylor slammed a fist on the table. "God damn it! The Army's got into the fray!"

Captain Jack said, "they might be Green Berets from Fort Carson. Or perhaps a Long Range Reconnaissance Patrol?"

"Drop a missile," said Snoopy Taylor, "let's see if we can flush some quail."

A Predator drone glided over the ranch and launched a missile into Joe Lucky's meadow, and then went floating off into the sun. There was a huge explosion. The earth spit up clods of dirt and grass. LRRPS popped up like gophers from under layers of sod, fired some rapid bursts from M16's, and then sank back down into the earth.

Joe Lucky, Rachel and Summer ran out of the house and stood in the yard. In the distance they saw a plume of smoke linger in the air. Joe Lucky shielded his eyes and looked up into the sun.

"What the hell was that?" he said in bewilderment.

"Joe, are they bombing us?" asked Rachel.

"The government wouldn't bomb us."

"The government bombs everybody, Joe."

She grabbed Summer and went back into the house, slamming the porch door for effect. Joe Lucky walked to the barn, dark with gloom. He unshackled the heavy chains on the double doors and walked inside to gaze upon his shiny, slumbering flying saucer.
    And then he saw sunlight pouring through the
        hole in the roof. He climbed up the ladder
            and onto the UFO and gazed up
              into the gaping hole. "It looks
                like I got some nasty
                  skunks on the
                    premises."

CHAPTER NINETEEN

"MERTHA!"
SAID ORTEGA.
Citizens were huddled up at the church. San Miguel was in riot mode again, protesting the military in their air space. They tolerated the Texas doves, but they would not tolerate the military.

Ortega pulled up behind Pachuco's truck in his dusty Dodge Ram. He spoke through his loudspeaker phone.

"Don't you people have jobs?"

The crowd turned their wrath toward Ortega. Dino Gonzales, a fifty-year old trouble-maker, who had a small potato farm down by the Conjeos River, was hoping to stir up more discontent.

"Ortega, you need to go get that flying saucer and give it to the government!" He spat a brown stain of tobacco on the ground. "Those pinche planes are getting on my nerves."

"That's right," said a voice from the crowd, "trade the damn thing for some government grants."

"Hey," someone said, "we can all weave rugs like comadre Lucy Gonzales with some looms. I think they will give grants for weavers."

"How about this," Ortega said into his loudspeaker, "Dino can start a stud ranch with his plow horse. How about that for a grant? Or Pachuco can become a wine taster for grape growers in California. Que no?"

"How about we get a grant to start a recall for our sheriff?" Dino said. There was a chatter of agreement.

"Whatever Joe Lucky has in the barn is my concern," said Ortega, "I'm still the law in San Miguel."

"What law?" asked Max.

"Borracho Pete Mestas locks himself in jail every Saturday," added Dino. "And where are you? Getting some tail! The last arrest you made was the Lovato boys for waxing windows on

Halloween."

Ortega stepped out of the truck, and he pulled his baseball cap down to his squinting eyes. He was at the end of his rope. He toyed with his big revolver on his hip. "As I recall, I was elected to this position by all of you."

"Well, none of us ever made the dean's list," Max said. "That ain't saying much."

"Where's Pachuco?" asked Ortega.

"He's with Padre Gomez. Honk your horn," said Felicia Velarde, a big boned woman with a straw hat and colorful blouse.

Ortega leaned into the window of his truck and honked the horn. Father Padre came out of the church, leading a contrite Pachuco.

"Oh lord," said Felicia, "I think he peed his pants, pobrecito. He smells ripe."

"What are you going to do to him?" asked Max.

"Take him home," said Ortega.

"He won't go home," said Dino. "An evil spirit is there. And Casper, too."

Father Gomez surrendered the shotgun to Ortega, who cracked open the breech and looked for shells. He tossed the shotgun into his truck.

"Tread lightly," warned Max, "the old viejo is a war hero."

"That's right," added Dino, "and now everything has gone to hell because of that goddamn Joe Lucky."

Pachuco sobbed. "They were killing my chickens."

"We should kill Joe Lucky and his cow," said Felicia.

"Too late for that, Felicia," added Max. "Flying saucer sliced the cow in half. And that bullshit you said about what goes up must come down. Kiss my ass, Ortega."

Ortega took charge of Pachuco.

"Are you arresting the viejo for refusing to go home?" asked Max. The crowd stirred.

"So now you're throwing us in jail," said Dino. "For nothing!"

"I'm going to lock him up for his safety," Ortega said. He placed Pachuco inside the truck. They drove thirty feet to the jail directly across the street.

The San Miguel jail was a blue matchbox, inside and out.

It contained one cell with a toilet and a shower stall at the end of a blue hallway. There was a wooden chair in the hallway as a point of observation for dangerous criminals in the cell.

There were not many criminals to lock up. The great trout fishing on the Conjeos and Rio Grande, and the famous sand dunes brought in the summer tourists. In the winter, he had few customers. The elk season always put the citizens in a frenzy because private landowners charged exorbitant prices for the hunts. Of course, this excluded the locals, who considered the forests and the land as their own, by virtue of ancient Spanish land grants. So as bullets whizzed at elk and deer and black bear, they also whizzed by the orange hats and vests of Texans and Okies and all hunters of unknown origin. Max was a faithful customer during the hunting season.

But Pachuco Pacheco was considered one of the dangerous culprits in San Miguel. Every first of the month, as predicable as the harvest moon, he would cash his VA check at The Lucky Strike Liquor Store and buy a gallon of Mescal and proceed to consume half of it at the city park. Snorting drunk, he would remove the shotgun from his truck and blast holes into the sky. Ortega was the only one who could talk to the old man. And when Ortega was out of town on poaching business, Pachuco just stumbled to the jail and locked himself in the cell.

"World War II is over, viejo," Ortega would gently say to Pachuco Pacheco. "The krauts are kaput. The Japanese too. Give me the gun, viejo, and we will go down to the jail and drink some of your wine."

Pachuco told him the stories about Iwo Jima and how thrifty and sneaky were the Japanese. And Ortega always reminded him that the Japanese farmers were upstanding citizens in the valley. Ortega and Pachuco consumed much of the wine before he sent the old man into the cell. He would always release him the next day.

It was standard police procedure with most of the citizens in San Miguel. Catch and release. Very much like the eighteen inch rule on the rainbows in the Conjeos River. Last night's episode was different. It was out of character for the old man. Something had scared the crap out of him. But things were really getting out of whack. What did Shakespeare say? What devious plots we weave. A lot of Shakespeare's people had the good sense to throw themselves onto their own sword. Or was that the Japanese?

Things were getting mucho malo. Soldiers were on the ground. Joe Lucky had something in his barn. And it was important enough for friend and foe to be dallying around in his meadow. He wondered if he should pull up stakes and go to Denver to become a real cop. Drive in a patrol car and look for taggers and don't give a hoot. He could even shoot some perp and nobody would be yelling for his cojones. A simple street cop. It had a good ring to it. . .because the only one getting shot down here, he mused, as he lifted the gallon jug to his quivering lips, was most likely, a Mr. Hector Ortega, Sheriff.

CHAPTER TWENTY

JOE
LUCKY
sat on top
of the UFO wearing
his goggles and holding
a chain saw. He looked up at
Snippy. "What do you think, Snippy?"
he asked, "are these the boys who did the
dirty deed on you?" Snippy clattered her bones
from a secret breeze. Joe Lucky pulled the starter cord
and the chain saw buzzed. He applied the blade to the UFO.

There was a terrible din and a shower of sparks. The chain saw went flying out of his hands and spun on the ground creating a dirt devil. Joe Lucky jumped off the UFO and circled the spinning saw. He attempted to grab the devilish thing without losing a limb. Sneaking behind the mad implement, he reached out and flicked off a switch. Then he heard a commotion in front of the barn. He opened the doors and looked through his goggles at thirty guns pointed at him. He still had the chainsaw in his hand. From the back of pickups, Max, Dino and other citizenry stared down Joe Lucky.

"Hola, Joe. Que pasa?" asked Max, wearing his 101st Airborne Screaming Eagle shirt. A front pocket boasted a deer knife.

"Hello, Max. You come to hunt some jackrabbits?"

"Jackrabbits! What you got in the barn?" Max pointed his 30-30 rifle directly at Joe Lucky.

"Old Snippy," said Joe Lucky. "Admission is still one dollar."

"Who gives a damn about a dead horse?" someone said.

"Yeah! And who you supposed to be? Leather face from puto Texas?" asked Dino.

"I wouldn't mind chopping off a few legs and arms," said Joe Lucky.

"You take one step toward me," said Max "and I'll blow a

hole in you so big Corky Cortez can drive his Toyota through it."

"We heard through the grapevine, Joe," said Dino. "You got a flying saucer."

"What grapevine?" asked Joe Lucky.

"Pablo Gomez heard it from Steve Vigil who heard it from that gringo boy who is banging the sheriff's daughter. That you found a flying saucer," explained Dino. "That grapevine, cabron!"

"And it killed your cow and drank the milk," someone offered.

"Toots? Yes, Toots passed to the great pasture in the sky," Joe Lucky said.

Dino cocked his rifle. Joe Lucky dropped the saw and ran into the barn. He came out with his own 30-ought-six."We got us a Mexican stand off," he said.

"We're the Mexicans," said Max. "You're the only standoff."

Rachel came running across the yard and directly into the fray. "What's going on?" She stepped in front of Joe Lucky and spread her arms like bird wings.

"We want the flying saucer," someone demanded.

"And I want a DVD of ET, the extra terrestrial," said Joe Lucky. "I want a lot of things."

"Play with fire and you get burned," warned Max.

"Max, you will have to shoot me too," said Rachel, defiantly. She pointed to her ample breast. "Are you up to shooting a woman?"

"We don't shoot women," said Dino. "But the army might. Renaldo Chavez was in his hay field and saw soldiers falling from the sky."

"You know what they say, Max," offered Joe Lucky. "Only birdshit and fools fall from the sky."

"Yes," Max agreed, "but that birdshit splattered down right onto your ranch, pendejo."

"I suggest you all go home," interceded Rachel, "and Joe and I will think about it."

"I already thought about it," said Joe Lucky. "I have no flying saucer. I have no little green men from Mars. And if I had either machine or man from outer space, I wouldn't give them to a bunch of lunatics."

Guns cocked. Nostrils flared.

"Let's not go off the deep end here!" Max suggested.

"Good thinking, Max, 'cause you would get my first volley."

At that moment a fighter jet streaked across the sky and disappeared over Panocha Ridge. Everyone looked skyward in expectation.

Dino removed his cap and whacked his thigh. "It's getting so bad all we do is look up into the sky. Let's go to Ducky's Bar for a cold cerveza and talk about this crisis," he said.

The trucks rolled off. Joe Lucky flipped the bird. Rachel went back to the house, as exasperated as the citizens. Joe Lucky went into the barn, sat on his cot and removed a bottle of Jack Daniels from under the pillow on his cot.

He drank long and hard and his belly was as warm as his emotions.

"Damn nuts," he muttered.

Ducky's Bar had a neon duck waddling across the roof of the tavern. On the edge of town it was the harbor for the long and lonely nights in the San Miguel valley. Ducky Garza took over the bar's ownership when his father died at eighty. He basically ran the same operation of free nachos with cheese and slices of jalepenos with his ice cold beer. When he could get it, he served the Mexican tequila with the puckered little worm on the bottom of the bottle. The bar had a jukebox with Mexican and American music, and there was a pool table in the middle of the room. A huge portrait of Emile Zapata hung behind the bar with the words:

"I WOULD RATHER DIE ON MY FEET THAN LIVE ON MY KNEES."

And they lived by Zapata's words. They were a spunky lot. They were kind and good people, but very headstrong in taking traditions to the grave. The people had developed its unique character in juxtaposing Native American beliefs with the Catholic church's piety. They were clannish and very superstitious, wary of outsiders and interlopers--especially gringos, and their simple ways contained myths and magical legends. They saw air ships buzzing in their valley and caught a glimpse of Bigfoot in the forests and choppers chasing fireballs across the sky. Simply said, there was some weird shit going on in the San Miguel Valley.

And this gentle way of loving the earth, respecting the elders, holding a great fatalist resilience in setbacks and sorrows in their songs and stories, rejoicing in births, copiously grieving in deaths. . .all this was protected from the modern world by the impenetrable mountains.

So imposing were these mighty ranges that Alferd Packer led a five man party into them in the spring of 1874, got hopelessly lost, ran out of provisions, and promptly ate heaping portions of all five men. Keeping up with the politics of the area, Judge M.B. Gerry sentenced Packer to be hanged and he supposedly proclaimed at the conclusion of his murder trial:

"There were seven democrats in Hinsdale County and you ate five of them, God damn you."

Ducky was so inspired by this famous event that he hung a portrait of Alferd Packer in the men's head, not fitting to hang with Zapata. Ducky was a devoted Democrat, as was the whole valley. And so Ducky, a small, wiry Hispanic, wiped his bar and said, "now tell me, why does Joe Lucky want to cause as much trouble as Alferd Packer?"

"I don't know," said Max. "He always was a trouble maker."

"Yeah, I remember the dirty trick he played on you," said Ducky. "The one during the football game."

Max choked up some of his Corona beer.

He said, "I hope those aliens hang that bastard on his barn rafter next to Snippy. I'd pay a dollar to see that."

The crowd at the bar hooted. CIA Bill entered and sat at a corner table under an enormous elk rack.

"Hombre, what can I get you?" asked Ducky.

"Scotch on the rocks," said CIA Bill. He removed his cowboy hat and observed his poison pin. He might have to prick somebody.

"Scotch?" said Dino. "Nobody drinks Scotch in San Miguel."

Ducky brushed off a dusty bottle and served the drink to CIA Bill.

The jukebox played Roberto Griego's version of "Wasted Days and Wasted Nights." The crowd at the bar lapsed into melancholy. Julie One Owl entered Ducky's. She looked hot as a tamale in tight jeans and low-cut T-shirt.

"Hola," she greeted the patrons.

"Hola," said the patrons in chorus.

"Maybe Joe doesn't have the UFO?" said Ducky.

"Why would the Army come down here where we have more rabbits than people?" inquired Dino.

"Testing secret weapons," suggested Frank Aguilar. He worked for Max when there was any work at the repair shop.

"They got Pinon Canyon for testing," Ducky speculated.

"Yeah," said Julie One Owl with bitterness in her voice, "and the Army wants more land down there too. They need more scrimmage room to practice for their conflicts. Those poor ranchers are gonna lose their land, just like we did."

'Well, they are here now," said Bert Romero, a large man with huge hands who raised goats on a tiny farm by the apple orchard. "But I don't believe Casper fell from the sky on a giant mushroom like Pachuco Pacheco swears."

"Pachuco didn't see any mushrooms," retorted Max, "he must be eating them."

"Si," said Dino, "Pachuco is so afraid he's living in his truck by the church. He won't go home. Julie One Owl has been taking him tacos and tamales. Isn't that so?"

"Pobrecito," said Julie One Owl. "What else can I do?"

Ducky twisted open a bottle top and served a beer to Julie One Owl.

"You'll see," said Max, "Ortega will arrest him for loitering."

"I don't think Ortega is against us," said Frank. "He's got a rule book to follow."

"Not only is his skin brown," retorted Max, "but he is a brown-noser too."

"The law has never stepped to our side of the fence," Ducky said sadly. "We all went to jail when we protested about the mountain. Where was the rule book on that one?"

"Good point, Ducky," praised Max. "Rich bastards come into the valley and buy the land we owned since the Spanish land grants. Then we can't hunt or harvest or cut timber on our own land where the bones of our ancestors rest." He paused to tame his emotions. "And I fought for this country. Did my time in 'Nam. They send boys off to get killed, shot and sick. Then a Vet files for benefits and they drag the claim on forever, hoping he'll die. When he dies, they dish out twenty bucks for a flag to put on top of his coffin." Max wagged his head like a dog with a tick in its ear.

"PTSD is not the present issue here," said Julie One Owl.

"The hell it ain't!" said Max. "It will be an issue when I go postal!"

CIA Bill took in this entire rancor about the government. He had a few issues himself with the system. Hell, if he died in this skirmish, his carcass would be tossed in a hole with no flag or trumpet. He sipped his scotch taking in this juicy revolution.

"I thought the Air Force was farting around down here?" someone said. "Not the Army."

"They got spy planes you know," said Julie One Owl. She sipped on her beer.

"Spy planes?" Dino repeated.

"Planes to take pictures," answered Julie One Owl.

"So?" said Dino.

"How do you supplement your incomes?" Julie One Owl motioned for a shot of tequila. Ducky poured her one. She sprinkled some salt on her hand, licked the salt, downed the shot, and said, "Well?"

Dino held out his arms. He didn't get it. Nobody did.

"Mota, pendejos!" said Julie One Owl, "Wacky weed. Each of you got a merry plot of Mary Jane growing down by the Conjeos River. Spy planes will see them."

The patrons fell silent. Max coughed falsely. Ducky poured shots for everyone. There was no sound but the tinkle of bottle on shot glass.

All eyes turned to CIA Bill, sitting beneath the seven-point elk rack. "Who is the gringo?" Dino inquired.
"A new plumber or something," muttered
Max. CIA Bill sensed ill feelings in the
air. He stood and lifted his scotch in
a toast. "Remember the Alamo!"
he shouted. "You lost
at the Alamo!"
retorted
Max.

CHAPTER TWENTY-ONE

DUKE
HAD ISSUES.
He wiped a paw at
his big black snout inside
the dog house. The death of
Toots had adversely affected his
emotional state. He missed Toots. He
could never get to Toot's dander, no matter
how much he barked at her. She liked to rest in the
grass and swish away flies with her tail. The ranch had been a quiet, peaceful plot of God's green acre and a good place for him to romp and chase rabbits for sport.

Now, chaos had replaced order. He listened to the Porky Pig chime on the porch jingle in the night breeze. The house slumbered under a dull crescent moon. Then the leaves on the oak tree seemed to shimmer and shake in the moonlight. Suddenly the whole house started to vibrate. He exited the dog house and woofed a couple of barks.

Inside the kitchen, a cup hopped across the table until it shattered on the floor. The hands on the wall clock spun erratically. The cupboards opened and spat out cans of food. The microwave beeped. The whole house hummed like a tuning fork.

Summer's I-pod fish swam into Joe Lucky's bedroom, harping something about the blue ocean. Joe Lucky shot up in bed. Rachel stirred awake.

"Joe, what's wrong?"

"I don't know."

The I-pod fish disappeared under the bed. Joe Lucky and Rachel ran for Summer's bedroom. He smashed open the door and turned on the light. They looked in horror as Summer, clutching her big doll, sat rigidly in bed. The bed was suspended off the floor. Joe Lucky leaped onto the bed and it crashed down. Rachel leaned against the wall and slid down to the floor. She sat, trembling, her face ashen.

"What's happening?" she asked in a whisper.

"Daddy, the bed was dancing," Summer said.

"It was just a dream," said Joe Lucky.

He walked out of the house, and paced in the yard. He looked up into the heavens. There was a tranquil peace to the blinking of a thousand stars. Was he wrong to harbor the flying saucer? What was he doing? He looked toward the town and could see a faint light.

Sheriff Ortega was taking care of business. His wife, Shirley, squealed beneath him. Ortega was stark naked except for his cowboy boots.

"Oh, mi Corazon!" yelped Shirley, a plump woman with dark eyes and long black hair.

"Call me 'DADDY' when I'm in the saddle," said Ortega. He saw a bright light outside the bedroom window. He leaped off the bed.

"Don't stop now!" said Shirley.

Ortega looked out the window and noticed a burning cross in his front yard. He ran out of the house wearing just his cowboy boots and waved his big Colt pistol over his head. Ortega yanked the cross out of the ground and stomped on the flames. Sparks sailed upward into the starry heavens.

"Jesus!" he exclaimed. "What now? The KKK?"

Rachel was morose all morning. She fried eggs in the kitchen, spooning hot grease for a white film over the yellow yolks. She was still as mad and hot as the grease. Bacon sizzled in another pan. Summer sat at the table and moped in her chair. She wore a Peter Pan costume complete with translucent wings and a green pointy hat.

"I don't want eggs," she whined, "I want Fruit Loops."

Rachel grabbed a bowl, poured Fruit Loops into the bowl and then milk. Rachel kissed Summer on the top of her head.

"What's in that flying saucer, mommy?"

"God only knows, honey."

"Daddy says there's good in there."

"Well, you're daddy isn't thinking too clearly."

"What happened last night? Was it the little green men from Mars?"

"No, honey. I don't want you to be afraid. We'll get rid of that machine in the barn and things will be fine." She arranged eggs, bacon and toast on a plate and poured a glass of orange juice.

"I'm going to take daddy some breakfast," said Rachel.

Rachel saw Joe Lucky on top of the barn. He was hammering in the hot sun. She put the plate on the seat of the tractor.

"Come down and eat, Joe."

"Some weasel tried to get into the barn. I'll come down in a few minutes."

Rachel stood with hands on hips. "Ok Joe. I'll just bring plates of food to you like Duke. You can dine together."

"What's that supposed to mean?" Joe Lucky asked.

"It means you're in the dog house. It means I would like my husband to sit and eat at the table like a family once in a blue moon," she said. She walked back to the house and noticed Summer running into the meadow.

"Summer," she called, "be careful!"

Summer spun in circles genuflecting with her magic wand. A man popped up out of the tall grass. He sported sunglasses and a camouflage shirt and shorts. A long lens camera dangled around his neck.

"Hello, little girl," he whispered.

Summer stopped spinning. "I'm Peter Pan. I'm not supposed to talk to strangers."

"I'm not a stranger. I'm a reporter."

"Whatcha doing on my daddy's land?"

"I need to know what's in the barn.

"Why?"

"If you tell me, I can take your picture."

"Why do you need to know?"

"It's important for my story."

"What story?"

"You ask a lot of questions."

Summer anointed him with her wand.

"I want to put a story in the newspaper. Wouldn't that be neat? To read about your daddy in the newspaper."

Summer slowly approached. "He has something good."

"Something good?" repeated the man. "What?"

"A flying saucer," Summer said, spinning so hard that her Peter Pan hat almost sailed off.

"Dear me!" said the man.

Summer twirled off, giggling. The man crawled on all fours into the tall grass. He popped up in the distance like a prairie dog, and snapped photographs of Joe Lucky's barn in the distance.

CIA Bill popped up too. He observed the man and then sank back into the grass. He typed into his message machine: "It's getting complicated, fellow spooks. The shit is going to hit the fan and the AP."

He waited patiently in the grass, swatting at a cloud of mosquitoes. The text machine blinked back: "AP?"
CIA Bill typed: "Associated friggin' Press, idiots!" The text message blinked: "Buy the Cadillac." CIA Bill typed: "What's the ceiling?" The machine blinked: "One million." CIA Bill closed the machine. He exclaimed: "Are you kidding? You can buy the whole beanfield for a million bucks!"

CHAPTER TWENTY-TWO

DAWN
BROKE OVER
the San Juan Mountains.
Streaks of orange light reached
across the wine-dark sky. An old rusty
pickup smoked down Main Street. A boy in the
back of the truck pitched newspapers toward the facades
of the weary buildings. One bounced off the door of Julie One
Owl's cafe. She opened the door and picked up the newspaper. All quiet on the western front, she thought, as she glanced up and down the street.

Everything in San Miguel seemed sad and desolate. A few sleepy dogs curled up on the sidewalks. She went inside the cafe, poured herself a cup of coffee and sat at one of her colorful yellow oilcloth tables. She opened the newspaper.

"Oh madre!" she exclaimed, "that pinche Joe Lucky finally did it!" She slammed the newspaper on the table. On the front page there was a photograph of Joe's Lucky's house and barn, and above a headline that screamed:

"FLYING SAUCER CRASHES IN RANCHER'S MEADOW!"

She went to the front window and noticed a green
Hummer come down the street with
tiny American flags flapping
in the crispy air. She said,
sadly, "Here comes
World War
III."

CHAPTER TWENTY-THREE

AN
RV CRUISED
down Highway 160.
The sides were painted
with swirls of hippy designs
and mysterious Mayan symbols. It
sported a television antenna on top. Jimmy
Zoot, a hippie in his fifties, passed a joint to his
wife Claire. Jimmy wore a red bandanna on his forehead. Claire wore a yellow one, a ratty cotton dress and round sunglasses though it was night. Claire had met Jimmy when they were students at The University of Colorado during the turbulent sixties. They had a mutual love for literature, art and the paranormal. In their junior year, they were both expelled for their rabble-rousing protests against the Vietnam War. Relieved to be purged from the establishment, they set off to visit the Aztec ruins in Mexico. There, sitting on top of these wondrous stone temples, Jimmy and Claire attempted to make contact with alien forms. One night, extremely high on pot, Jimmy made contact with Herman Cortes and demanded to know why the Conquistador had demolished the great Aztec civilization. Cortes, the insolent scamp, removed his helmet and lofted his sword.

"Because I could," he told Jimmy.

The epiphany changed Jimmy for life. Civilization would destroy itself because it could. That was life's great mystery. Jimmy and Claire believed that the world would end with the Mayan calendar in 2012. The hippie couple returned to Colorado to wait for new signs. Time was short. And then they heard about Joe Lucky through the UFO grapevine.

Jimmy and Claire listened with inspiration to a UFO song by Creedence Clearwater. It was Jimmy's band of choice during the great protest years of bloody batons and smoke bombs. They sang along:

"Oh, it came out of the sky, landed just a little south of Alamosa. Joe Lucky fell out of his tractor, couldn't b'lieve what he seen."

Claire passed the joint back to Jimmy. He took a mighty toke. Then he glanced out the window and noticed the entrance gate to the J. Lucky Ranch. He yanked the wheel into a sudden U-turn. The RV skidded on screeching tires and nearly toppled. Jimmy dropped the roach into his lap. He beat his legs as if he had a bongo in his lap.

"There it is, Jimmy!" shouted Claire.

"I know! I know!"

The RV crashed through the railed fence. Jimmy reversed the RV and parked near the entrance gate. He jumped out and removed a ladder from the rear of the vehicle. He climbed on top of the RV. Claire looked up at him, losing him in the stars.

"We got a prime spot," he said, "fetch the telescope stuff."

Claire removed a long silver telescope and tripod and went up the ladder onto the roof. Jimmy assembled the telescope.

"Fire up a joint, peaches," he said, focusing the telescope on the big dark sky.

"I hope we brought enough food," she said, firing up the joint.

"No matter," said Jimmy. "I saw a food mart down the road in San Miguel."

She handed the joint to Jimmy.

"This is really a trip," he said in a gravel voice, sucking smoke and holding it deep in his lungs.

"Jimmy, we're on a mission," said Claire. "Let's sleep up here under the stars like old times."

"You damn right we're on a mission, peaches!" answered Jimmy.

The green Hummer rolled down Highway 160 following the Conejos River. Captain Jack was driving. Snoopy Taylor looked out at the vast valley.

"They claim we've got a top secret military base here in the mountains," Snoopy Taylor said.

"We might," said Captain Jack, "who knows anything? They see a lot of funny stuff in the sky and blame the military. There's a lot of strange magnetic pulls on the earth in this spot. It's a hotbed for UFO sightings. Some say it's just bad Ute medicine."

Snoopy Taylor noticed some trucks parked along the river. "Slow down," he ordered.

Next to the river, Max and Dino were unfurling camouflage sheets in the willow trees to cover their marijuana plots. The Hummer stopped on the highway. Max and Dino dived under the sheets. Snoopy Taylor unrolled his window for a better look.

"What they doing, Jack?"

"Fishing?" said Captain Jack. "I know that skinny one. That's Max Campos. Last time we came to the valley, he put sugar in our gas tanks. We were immobile for a week. Campos is a Vietnam Vet and all those Nam vets are crazy."

"Can we have him arrested?" inquired Snoopy Taylor.

"I doubt it. There would be a massive uproar."

Snoopy Taylor pondered.

"I'd like to get those alien bastards out of that capsule and choke them to death," he said. "I didn't have this much anxiety in Iraq." He rolled up the window and the Hummer accelerated down Highway 160.

Jimmy and Claire were sitting in lawn chairs in front of the RV when the Hummer pulled into the ranch entrance gate. Jimmy removed his sunglasses and said, "Looks like GI Joe knows what we know, Claire."

Claire waved happily at Captain Jack in the Hummer. The Hummer zoomed down the dirt road in a cloud of dust.

The Hummer pulled into the yard and Joe Lucky stepped out onto the porch. Captain Jack and Snoopy Taylor exited the Hummer and looked at Joe Lucky through sunglasses. Joe Lucky saw the glint of four silver stars on Snoopy's broad shoulders.

"Joe Lucky?" asked Snoopy Taylor.

"That's me. But I never been lucky, sir."

"Today might be a lucky one for you, my boy," said Snoopy

Taylor. "I'm General Taylor from NORAD, son. This is Captain Jack. Did you know some hippies just crashed through your fence?"

"Probably smoking weed," said Joe Lucky. "There's a lot of pot in the valley. That's why everybody sees so many flying saucers."

"We have some questions to ask," said Captain Jack. "Joe, we know something crashed on your ranch. Can you tell us about it?"

"Gentlemen, the only thing crashed on my ranch was a missile. And I'm betting the bank that you were the author of it."

Joe Lucky let loose with a shrill whistle. "Hey, honey! Can you bring us three lemonades? We got a four-star general here! Hell, that's more stars than I got in grade school!" He sat on the swing porch and looked at the two Air Force bluebirds.

"Now, son, you remember, try real hard" said Snoopy Taylor with a wink. "Tell us the truth."

Snoopy Taylor and Captain Jack went onto the porch and sat at the table, fanning themselves with their Air Force hats.

"You know what they say," answered Joe Lucky, "if you tell the truth you don't have to remember."

Captain Jack removed his sunglasses. "We hear you're losing the ranch, Joe."

"That's a possibility."

Rachel carried out a tray of iced lemonade and glasses. She put the tray on the porch table. "No possibility, Joe," said Rachel. "We're in the potato patch with no shovel. Please listen to what they have to say."

Snoopy Taylor picked up a glass and drank heartedly. "It's been getting hot around here," he said.

"Hotter than a jalapeno," said Joe Lucky, "and we haven't reached the seedy part yet."

"Mrs. Lucky?" asked Snoopy Taylor.

Rachel nodded. Snoopy Taylor attempted to throw on the charm.

"I see you're the brains of this operation. You know, we can make that bank note on the ranch go away. Just turn over that Easter egg inside the barn."

"Simple as that," added Captain Jack. "It would be the patriotic thing to do."

"There's no Easter egg in my barn," said Joe Lucky. He felt a rush of exaltation. He was proud of his civil disobedience.

"We could throw in a shiny new tractor," Captain Jack said.

"A new tractor wouldn't do me any good," replied Joe Lucky. "I have no seeds to sow. I have no hay fields to harvest. And I have no cattle to eat the hay."

"Yeah," said Rachel, "it's like the Grapes of Wrath around here."

Snoopy Taylor became irate, turning boiled lobster red. "Listen, son, we can toss in a cash bonus and maybe a couple of tickets to Thailand. If you just leave the barn door open when you depart the premises."

Rachel crossed her arms, equally irate. "Joe, we never had a honeymoon."

"I know, baby," Joe Lucky said sadly. He paced the porch. He stopped and looked over his meadow and beyond to Panocha Ridge. "I'm sorry, gentlemen. No use chappin' my ass. I must say adios amigos."

Snoopy Taylor smacked his hat on the porch pillar. "Let's go, Jack." They ambled off for the Hummer. Duke shot out of the dog house and pissed on the Hummer's front tire in his own act of treason. He went back inside his house.

"Don't mind the dog," said Joe Lucky. "He's got some emotional problems."

Snoopy Taylor and Captain Jack boarded the Hummer and roared out of the yard. Rachel sat wearily at the table. She looked up at her husband with despair in her blue eyes.

"Why don't they just come in here and take the damn thing? And kill us in the process," she asked.

"Waco," said Joe Lucky.

"Waco?"

"They can't kill me now. They should have whacked me on the first day. I bet they're crying about that right now. They would have to kill Summer and you and the whole valley to make a clean sweep under the rug."

"What a comforting thought," said Rachel. "Didn't they take that flying saucer in Roswell?"

"Sure did, honey. But claimed it was a weather balloon. They'll deny everything. Government's policy is to tell lies and deny."

"What do you intend to do, Joe?"

"I don't know."

In the Hummer, Snoopy Taylor stared grimly at the red phone on the dash. Captain Jack drove in silence. They passed through the entrance gate. He looked out the window. He saw Jimmy Zoot still in his lawn chair. Claire wore a floppy chef's hat and flipped smoking hamburgers on a grill. Occasionally, she toked on a joint.
Snoopy Taylor said, "It's going to turn into a freak show, Jack." He picked up the phone. "Mr. President," he said with regret in his hoarse voice, "we have a problem."

CHAPTER TWENTY-FOUR

SAN MIGUEL was as quiet as a graveyard. Birds sang from the church belfry. Julie One Owl watched a field mouse run helter-skelter from Bertha's Antique Store to the Sheriff's office. Pachuco Pacheco had pitched a canvas over the back of his pickup at the church and was hibernating. A yellow school bus, packed with old people, rambled up the street and parked in front of the cafe. Spunky senior citizens exited the bus. Some of them had binoculars around their necks like bird watchers. They sported colorful baseball caps. Two were very old and supported themselves on hickory canes. They filed by Julie One Owl and into the cafe. Julie One Owl watched them fill up her tables. They were excited and jabbering like magpies. Julie One Owl passed out menus.

"Welcome to San Miguel," she told a trio--one man and two women-- who sported black horn-rimmed glasses. "I hope you enjoy the town of San Miguel. It's the oldest town in Colorado."

They looked up at her like owls.

"We didn't come to see San Miguel," the old man said.

"Why would we?" said the first woman. "You have more goats than people."

"Why did you come, may I ask?" Julie One Owl removed a pencil from her hair and prepared to take orders.

"Dear, we come to see the flying saucer ranch!" said the second woman.

"You know, beat the crowds," said the man.

"You mean more will come?" asked Julie One Owl in astonishment.

"Of course, dear," said the first woman, "don't you know what you got? My lord, not even the Smithsonian has a flying saucer. What's the special today, dear?"

"Let's see," said Julie One Owl. "I have the Star Trek burger that is topped with green chili and the famous flying saucer curly fries."

The trio was delighted.

"We'll have those!" said the man.

Thomas was snoring on his cot when Julie One Owl entered and shouted from the prep table. "Thomas! We got some customers!"

Thomas shot up from his cot. He rubbed sleep from his eyes. "We never have customers," he complained.

"We do now, pendejo! I need 27 burgers with green chili and 27 curly fries."

Thomas put on a stained apron, ambled to the refrigerator to get frozen patties and then fired up the old grill. In a moment, hamburgers were sizzling. Julie One Owl filled glasses of ice water. Thomas flipped a row of hissing burgers. "Who's out there?" he asked. "The Mexican Army?"

CHAPTER TWENTY-FIVE

MAX
CAMPOS LAY
in his hammock next
to his marijuana patch and
listened to the Conjeos River giggling
like school girls as it passed his covert camp.
He had endured a hard night. Somewhere down river,
he heard a woman crying and knew immediately who was
wandering the river. His heart shriveled in his chest. And
at that moment, when the moon broke through a haze of clouds,
she nearly made him take flight with her cry.

It was La Llorona. The Weeping Woman. A woman who came in many forms. A virgin. A siren. A witch. A harlot. Max knew her well. His mother told him the story to scare the crap out of him as a child. La Llorona was better than a belt.

It started in Mexico, back in the early Colonial period. The myth passed through numerous modifications, but she was always the beautiful peasant woman who fell in love with a rich Spanish rancher. They wed and had two lovely children. The rancher grew tired of Maria's conceited ways and wanted to marry within his own class. He took a young beautiful señorita as a play toy. Maria, like any scorned woman, vowed revenge.

One day, by the river, some say the Río Grande, others say it happened near Mexico City, while she was walking with her children, he rode by in a wagon with the señorita at his side.

In a fit of jealous rage, Maria tossed the children into the swift currents of the river, and they were carried away into lore. She immediately realized what she had done. The most despicable act a parent can render upon a child. She drowned herself in the river and her spirit began to wander aimlessly near any waters, looking for her children, and crying out:

"Donde estan mis hijos?"

Her horrifying cry has passed through the centuries as timeless and irrevocable as the river. Spirits had very little preferences, and La Llorona was said to kill children, women and men.

Max put his pistol down on the ground because bullets would do no good against this lady of the waters. He took some comfort waiting on his hammock for the safety of the morning. He didn't think Mary Jane growers were very high on her pardon list.

And if she did come for him, he hoped it would be as a beautiful apparition. He didn't want to give up the ghost to some ugly bitch.

And then the sun came up, round and yellow as an egg yolk in the sky. Max swung to-and-fro in his hammock and listened to a coyote yelp down river. He looked lovingly at the Sangre de Cristo Mountains. The Spaniards had christened them for the awe-inspiring bloody red sunsets in her crown. Sangre de Cristo simply translated into "blood of Christ."

He watched the meadow larks zip through the light like sparks. He reached over to a radio on a rock and clicked on a voice:

"You're listening to KRFT in the valley. Remember ladies, get those pies for the prize down to the Dew Drop Community Center on Saturday. . ."

On the Conejos, a rainbow trout leaped up for a floating fly and then did a number ten dive back into the languid river. The radio voice, as if he had witnessed the leaping trout, said:

"The fishing has been great down on the Conejos. If you see a tourist tell him we got the best truchas in Colorado. In other news, there have been reports of aliens abducting dogs and eating chickens. That's right, chickens and not the Kentucky Fried pollos, mi amigos. Joe Lucky please give up the machine, my man. . ."

Max swung off the hammock. He attempted to adjust the radio for better reception. The voice said:

"This song goes out to Joe Lucky down on the ranch. Mi amigo, we're stuck in the middle with you. . ."

And the lyrics of a song hammered home his symbolic words:

"Well I don't know why I came here tonight. I've got a feelin' that something' ain't right."

Max issued a volley of curses.

He clicked off the radio. He paced his camp. Sunlight poured onto the land, and the crickets had ceased their courting songs.

Max picked up a hose dipped into the river. He sucked mightily and began to water his four-foot marijuana plants.

In Joe Lucky's meadow, the LRRP's had climbed out of their foxholes and retreated quietly into the dawn to a small Army camp on the sacred mountain. The camp, covered in nets of green camouflage, had all the goodies of field communications. Antennas turned on top of the air-conditioned trailers. Teletype machines clattered from inside one trailer. Sgt. Stanley Reemes, a handsome boy from Boston, led his hungry LRRP's to a cooking tent where they could stress-down with cigarettes and coffee.

A LRRP turned on his pocket radio and listened to a voice on KRFT:

". . .Pendejos to the left of me, hecklers to the right. Here I am stuck in the middle with you. . ."

The LRRP's played cards on a table.

"Sgt Reemes," said a Spec-4, "what are we waiting and watching for?"

"Hell," said Reemes. "I don't know. Just watch."

A cook in a white apron approached. "Breakfast boys?" he asked.

"Yeah," said the Spec-4, "but leave out that hamburger gravy."

The cook laughed and wiped his brow with his dirty apron.

"What's the matter, soldier," he said. "You don't like my shit on a shingle?"

On the porch, Joe Lucky and Rachel sat on the swing in the evening light sipping ice tea. It was that moment of dusk when everything stands still and sounds soar for miles.

A dog barked somewhere in the valley. An owl hooted mysteriously from Panocha Ridge. Up in the heavens bright stars winked in the purple sky.

Look at the Milky Way, honey," said Joe Lucky.

"I see it," Rachel said.

"Now we know there's life up there. I wonder if we came from there too."

"We came from our parents, Joe. You know, sex. Like how we made Summer. You know, like how we seem to lack in our lives at the present time."

"I mean spiritually, not in the physical realm."

"We're in the physical realm right now," said Rachel. "I'm just hoping we don't get a bullet between the eyes. This moment. Present time."

"Baby the Army is gone."

"I'm not talking about the Army, Joe. I'm talking about the locals."

"You mean Max and his compadres? They just talk a lot of hot sauce." He hugged Rachel.

"Joe?"

"Yeah, honey."

"I hope there's a God."

"Me too," said Joe. "It would be a shame to waste all that singing in church. I pray just in case there is a God, kind of like having State Farm Insurance."

"What if there's no heaven?"

"That's OK," said Joe Lucky. "I'm in heaven right now with you."

Rachel kissed him. "You're charming for such a scamp, Joe."

"I read where the Vatican said that it's acceptable to believe in aliens because it does not contradict our faith in God."

"Joe, are you making that up?"

"No, honey. I read it in magazine. The director of the Vatican Observatory, a Reverend Jose Funes, said that in the vastness of the universe there could be other intelligent life outside of earth."

"Boy, they got that right," said Rachel.

"He said such a notion doesn't contradict faith because aliens would still be God's creatures? And ruling out the existence of aliens would be like putting limits on God's creative freedom." "And the Pope didn't defrock this reverend?" asked Rachel. "I don't recall the Pope saying anything about the reverend or the aliens. There has to be a reason the flying saucer crashed on our ranch." "Because it ran out of gas?" offered Rachel."

CHAPTER TWENTY-SIX

CIA
BILL LAY
on the bed. He was
in the second floor of Tita's
Bed and Breakfast Inn. He sported
blue boxers and white knee-length socks.
He missed his wife, Wilma, on these projects and
wished he was out of this potato patch in Colorado. He
gazed up at the ceiling fan which swished like a helicopter
blade. He had been in the CIA for twenty-two years and had
never been elevated above the dreary third floor at Langley. At
fifty-five he was still a field spook and his future was bleak at
the agency. What could he do? Take the company's million
bucks and catch a plane for Cambodia? He could live in a
Buddhist temple and proclaim himself king of the jungle like
Marlon Brando in that flick? But what good would a million
bucks do there? He would just be Lord of the Monkeys.

    Still that prospect seemed better than this prissy one. He
snatched a bottle of scotch and took a big swig.
He went to the window. A couple of
tourists were milling below in
the garden. Two doves cooed
in the plaza's tree.
"Annoying little
bastards," he
said.

CHAPTER TWENTY-SEVEN

SUMMER
WAS PLAYING
in a dreamland. The
bedroom was filled with
childish things, including a pink
dresser with a child's funny-face clock
on top. Next to the clock the I-pod fish lay
beached and quiet. The big doll slumped in a child's
rocker, two arms hanging limply over the sides. Summer hugged a teddy bear. Stuffed animals reposed in every corner, glassy eyes staring into infinity.

Suddenly, the I-pod fish sang out: "Come with me to the big blue sea. . ." and at this outburst the clock ticked to a dead stop. Summer stirred in bed. The doll started to rock in the chair, creaking on the hardwood floor, and then the doll opened big blue eyes. The doll's head turned to look at Summer.

Click. Click. Two shoes hit the floor and rapidly clicked across the room. The door squeaked open. Summer heard the door and sat up in bed. She looked around the room and noticed that the doll was gone.

"Sarah?" she called.

Summer ran out of the bedroom. The fish did a head dive and swam on the floor. In the living room the television raced through channels in a white ghostly glow to finally settle on a wacky cartoon of Woody Woodpecker. Summer ran barefoot into the yard. She stood in her Winnie The Pooh pajamas.

"Sarah? Where are you?"

Rachel awoke in a fright. She went to the window and heard Summer giggling in the yard.

"Summer?" she called. "Joe get up!"

Summer stared at the barn. Joe Lucky and Rachel ran out of the house. Rachel slowly turned her giggling daughter to look in her face. Summer had a strange lost expression. Rachel went pale.

"Summer are you OK? What's wrong honey?" She
took Summer in her arms. "Sarah can walk and talk, mommy."
"Where is Sarah, honey?" asked Rachel, afraid of the answer.
"She went to play with her friends." Summer pointed
to the barn. "Oh my God!" uttered Rachel. She
picked up Summer and ran into the house.
Joe Lucky looked at the house. The glow
of the TV and the wacky cartoon
music floated out into the yard.
He heard Duke whimpering
from inside the dog house.
He sat next to Duke.
"I hear you, boy,"
said Joe
Lucky.

CHAPTER TWENTY-EIGHT

CIA
BILL'S
battered truck
rattled down Highway 160.
He did a double take at the road
sign for the Yamoto Alligator Farm. A
dirt road made a straight dash through the
flatlands of blooming purple buds of cacti. He
wondered why the hell somebody was raising alligators
in the high desert. A sweet smell of sage blew into his open window. Sometime, he would have to stop and see this alligator farm. Tita, the owner of the bed and breakfast, had told him that there were many Japanese farmers in the valley. Maybe the Japanese were raising alligator to make those expensive boots for women. He could pick up a pair of alligator boots for Erma. Back at the bunker in Langley, they said this valley was the queen of paranormal activities. It was a very strange place, thought CIA Bill. Why are space crafts zipping through the thin Colorado air down in this potato patch? And why were people seeing Bigfoot, and why are people seeing immense fireballs chased by military choppers? Or seeing ghosts and demons? Man, he thought, this was a really weird place.

CIA Bill patted a black satchel bag on the seat.

He turned at the entrance to the J Lucky Ranch. He stopped and looked over the Zoot RV. Claire was hanging laundry on Joe Lucky's fence. He noticed the telescope on the vehicle's roof.

"Here come the UFO nuts!" he said, and accelerated for the distant ranch.

Joe Lucky was planting trip wires when CIA Bill pulled up.

"Howdy," said CIA Bill from the truck.

"Howdy yourself," said Joe Lucky.

"You got coyotes?"

"More than I can count."

Joe picked up a stake from his wheelbarrow and hammered

it into the ground. He wrapped the wire around the stake and pulled it taunt.

"Can I talk to you and your wife?"

Joe Lucky stood up. He looked closely at CIA Bill and his C&H Plumbing logo on the truck. "I ain't got any plumbing problems," he said, "unless you consider my enlarged prostate."

"Right now, plumbing is not the issue," said CIA Bill. He debarked with the black sachet bag. "My uncle from Denver delivered this bag of goodies last night. Let's go into the house."

Rachel poured coffee. Joe Lucky and CIA Bill looked at the bag on the table.

"I want to buy the machine in the barn," said CIA Bill.

"Why?" asked Joe Lucky.

"Because we want it?"

"Who wants it? C&H Plumbing?" asked Joe Lucky.

"Doesn't matter who wants it. That's not important. This is what is important," CIA Bill opened the satchel bag and spilled stacks of bills onto the table.

Rachel sat, her mouth open in astonishment. She picked up a stack of bills. "Joe, these are hundred dollar bills!"

CIA Bill said, "last time I counted, there was a million bucks in that bag."

Joe Lucky said, "turds must be a profitable business. I should have been a plumber, honey."

"You'll be set for life." CIA Bill picked up a stack. "Million bucks. Tax free and screw the IRS!"

Joe Lucky paced the kitchen.

"You can smoke Cuban cigars," said CIA Bill. "You can have a house on the Florida keys. College for the kiddie. A Porsche for the missie. A bone for the dog."

Joe Lucky stopped and pondered.

"Think of it, Joe," said CIA Bill in a velvet voice.

"Joe, let's go outside," said Rachel. "I want to talk to you."

They went onto the porch. CIA Bill drummed his fingers on the table. He could hear Joe Lucky and Rachel in a heated discussion. He smiled. Nothing got the juices flowing more than money. Rachel and Joe returned. CIA Bill tried to read their faces, but both looked annoyed. Rachel went to the sink and washed dishes.

"Tell me something," Joe Lucky said. "Where did you get this kind of money?"

"I have an uncle named Sam," said CIA Bill.

"What would you do with the machine if I did sell it?"

"Can't say, exactly. That's not my department."

"It wouldn't be good for the machine and the things inside the machine, would it?" asked Joe Lucky.

"Can't say. Don't know how to answer that," said CIA Bill.

"Well tell your uncle that I can't say either."

"Are you sure about this, Joe?"

"Positive," Joe Lucky said. CIA Bill put the stacks of bills into the black bag. "I'm staying at Tita's. Let me know if you change your mind." He departed. Joe Lucky sat chagrined at the table. Why did he turn down a million bucks? Why didn't he take the money? And run? Right out of this old exhausted valley. Rachel continued to wash dishes, but he could tell that she was crying. He heard CIA Bill cranked up the truck and roared away. Meekly, Joe Lucky walked out of the house and into the yard and returned to his wire snares.

CHAPTER TWENTY-NINE

THE
UFO NUTS
had arrived all
morning. There were new
and old trucks with campers. RV's
of all sizes and vans and station wagons.
There were a couple of motorcycles and one small
airplane. There was even a black Hearse with dreary
funeral flags. There were old and young people. Sane and
insane people. They all came to the J. Lucky Ranch and parked
their vehicles along the fence and then in rows. Someone had
tied up pear-shaped alien balloons onto the entrance gate and
they bobbled in the breeze. Kids sprinted everywhere, followed
by pursuing dogs and even a pet raccoon. Tables were set on
the ground and a hundred telescopes leaned against Joe Lucky's
fence. On the other side of the fence, kids were flying colorful
kites with long fluttering tails. A woman washed clothes on an
old fashion scrubbing board. Others were grilling hotdogs and
hamburgers and chicken and steaks. Two men struggled to
drop a keg of beer into a big tub of ice. Soon beer was foaming
into plastic cups, and voices took on a more boisterous tone.

Inside the RV, Jimmy puffed on a water bong stocked with pungent Mexican pot. He coughed up half his lungs. "Damn, that's some good mota," he said.

Claire was reading a Good Housekeeping magazine. She looked up at Jimmy. "Baby," she said, "do you think Joe Lucky is a messenger from the heavens?"

"Maybe not the messenger but the message."

"I'm just happy the people are coming," she said. "We must build a new cathedral at this place. Maybe a temple like in Mexico.
You remember when you talked to the ghost of
Cortes. And how he warned that the end of
mankind was near. The Rapture is coming.

And from here, the bells will ring out to all of mankind."
Jimmy sucked and water gurgled inside the
pipe. He held the smoke deep inside
his lungs. He exhaled and his
right eyeball rolled around
like the steel ball in a pin-
ball machine. "Man,
I can't wait for the
mother ship,"
Jimmy
said.

CHAPTER THIRTY

ALAMA
WAS ABOUT
sixty miles from
San Miguel. It was the
biggest town in the valley
and was created by the agriculture
of thrifty Japanese and German farmers.
Potatoes helped the town grow enough for the
railroad to lay track across miles of high desert, and big enough to establish a college of some renown. Alama had made the big time. It even had a Red Lobster.

So when a four star general and his sidekick captain parked the Hummer in front of the State Bank & Trust and walked into the lobby, nobody gawked. Snoopy Taylor asked a teller to see the bank president, a Mr. William Goff II. The flyboys were ushered into the plush office of a fifty-year old man in an Italian silk suit. He wore bifocals and his grey hair was combed back at the sides, neat and slick as turtledove wings. He rose behind his desk to greet his guests.

"Good day, gentlemen," he said politely. "Please have a seat."

Snoopy Taylor and Captain Jack sat in plush velvet chairs.

"Hello, Mr. Goff," said Snoopy Taylor. "I'm General Taylor from up the road at NORAD and this is my liaison officer Captain Jack Holloway. We need to see the paperwork on a Mr. Joe Lucky. I would appreciate if you would keep this discreet."

"I can't do that, sir," said Goff. "I'm sorry but that is against the law."

"Now listen, Goff, we got TOP SECRET, NATO, SEATO, CRYPTO clearances," boasted Snoopy Taylor, "and we can damn sure see anything."

"We need to see material on Joe Lucky for security reasons," said Captain Jack.

Snoopy Taylor looked proudly at his sidekick. "That's right, this Lucky character might be involved in terrorist activities."

"Joe Lucky from San Miguel?" Goff asked in surprise.

"That's the one," answered Snoopy Taylor.

"Joe Lucky is a lot of things," said Goff, "but terrorist isn't one of them. He did blow up an outhouse with Billy Wagner sitting in it. But, hell, he was just a kid."

Goff went to a cabinet and removed a file. He sat down at his desk.

"Give us the lowdown," demanded Snoopy Taylor.

Goff cleared his throat. "Joe Lucky owes twenty thousand in back taxes for the ranch. And he's five payments behind on his ranch note."

"Boy," exclaimed Snoopy Taylor, "that randy woodpecker is in deep shit!"

"Can you confiscate the ranch?" asked Captain Jack.

"Gentlemen," said Goff, "our ranchers and farmers are the backbone of this valley. We give them all the chances within the law. We don't take anything until the last dog is hung."

"Mr. Goff," said Snoopy Taylor, "we just terminated the last dog. Now say you confiscate this J. Lucky Ranch, do all the personal items on said ranch get confiscated too?"

"I suppose so," Goff said, sadly.

"Well, Goff," snapped Snoopy Taylor, "I want you to pull that note on the ranch and put Joe Lucky out on his ass."

Goff walked to the window and watched two kids wearing bandannas on their foreheads spray paint "WAR MONGERS" on the side of the Hummer. He secretly smirked.

Snoopy Taylor removed a huge cigar, flicked his Bick, and blew a perfect smoke ring.

Down at the Conejos River, CIA Bill pulled off Highway 160 and parked on the Conejos bridge. He opened his text machine. By magic, a pistol was thrust into the window, and the barrel nudged into his left ear.

"I hope you're not the Son of Sam?" said CIA Bill.

"I don't hear any dog voices telling me who to shoot," said Max. "I'm the son of Mary Campos so I shoot what I want. What are you doing down here?"

"Taking a leak," said CIA Bill.

"You're the guy that was snooping around in Ducky's," said Max. "And Juan Gomez does the plumbing in San Miguel. Maybe you're a DEA agent?" Max poked harder with the pistol.

"Close, but no cigar, Pedro. I do the plumbing for the United States. I'm the one that flushes all the refuse down the toilet."

"My name ain't Pedro, cabron. What you got in the bag?"

"A million bucks."

"Yeah right, smart ass," Max said, losing his cool. "Now, vamos, before I put a bullet through your ear!"

CIA Bill's truck tires squealed off the bridge. Max blasted a round at the fleeing truck for encouragement.

Banker Goff was astonished. He sat in his new red Cadillac and was stuck in a traffic jam on Main Street of San Miguel. Vehicles were bumper to bumper from the city park to Emma's Convenience Store on the edge of town. Even the ancient Valdez Commons, the only commonlands in the United States to retain its original usage of communal grazing for cattle, was filled with parked automobiles. As usual, there was a protesting crowd in front of the sheriff's office. The natives were shouting about cattle being run off the commons by a gringo invasion.

Goff inched his Cadillac forward. Other drivers leaned on their horns. Goff saw a strange old man selling santos from the back of a battered pickup by the church. Indian women sat before tables of turquoise and silver jewelry. A man was selling candy apples and cotton candy from a push cart, ringing a bell to attract a hundred waifs. Julie's Cafe was bustling busy. A line waited at the entrance door where a sign proclaimed the Star Trek UFO burger and the flying saucer curly fries for $9.95. Goff traveled a hundred yards in forty minutes, and became as exasperated as the rest. He resorted to tooting his horn for passage. He finally reached Becky's Convenience Store, but getting gas was out of the question.

Becky was pumping more gas than Exxon.

Jimmy Zoot dipped into a barrel of Kentucky Fried Chicken and munched on a drumstick. The famous Colonel Sanders and Taco Bell were making deliveries from Alama for large orders. Jimmy took a bite out of a jalepeno and water came into his eyes.

"Ooooow, darlin', that was a hot one!" he said. He slurped on a straw inside his Coke can.

"Honey, pick me out some white meat," said Claire. They sat in lawn chairs in front of the RV. Jimmy handed her an extra-crispy breast. Classic rock music blared out of speakers on top of the RV. Across the fence, on Joe Lucky's land, women were sun bathing.

Goff stopped at the gate in his shiny new Cadillac. He removed two "FOR SALE" signs from the back of the automobile and nailed a sign on each side of the entrance gate. Jimmy and Claire approached, holding their pieces of chicken.

"Is Joe Lucky losing his ranch?" asked Jimmy.

"Looks that way," said Goff.

"You can't take his ranch!" protested Claire. "He's on a mission from God."

"Then I hope Joe Lucky can change water into wine," Goff said.

More people approached. An old woman with two sharp knitting needles said, "Do you want to bring the apocalypse upon us, you scalawag?" She made threat by poking her needles at Goff. Goff became uneasy and jumped into the automobile.

He sped off for Joe Lucky's ranch.

"My God, it's like a scene right out of the Twilight Zone," he muttered.

Joe Lucky puttered from his musty old hay stack to his barn. He was placing old bales of hay against the walls of his barn as a security procedure. Goff pulled into the yard and Joe Lucky puttered over to his Cadillac.

"Hello, Joe," Goff said, "I have some bad news. The bank is pulling your note."

"Mr. Goff," said Joe Lucky, "you promised me some time."

Goff exited and hammered a sign onto the barn door. "Bank wants to cut its losses. I'm sorry, Joe. I have to put up these signs."

"How much time do I have?"

"Thirty days."

Goff approached the house and nailed a sign onto the pillar of the porch. Rachel and Summer came out of house. "Sorry miss," said Goff, "I'm just a messenger." Rachel and Summer went into the yard and looked at the sign. "Mommy are we poor?" asked Summer, tears coming into her eyes. Rachel went down to her knees and looked directly into her sad face. "Don't cry, honey." Goff felt rotten. He went back to the Cadillac and left without another word. Joe Lucky sagged like a question mark on his tractor seat.

CHAPTER THIRTY-ONE

SHERIFF ORTEGA SAT with his cap in his hands inside the tiny San Miguel Courthouse. He waited to see Mayor Marty Salazar. The spunky Salazar, five-foot tall in his cowboy hat and boots, had won the mayorship by six votes. Some said he had voted twelve times for himself, and bought a lot of votes at Ducky's Bar.

"Bueno Dias, Sheriff Ortega," he said. "Entre."

Ortega went into his office and looked at the mighty mite.

"I want to resign," Ortega said. Ortega removed a letter of resignation and placed it on his desk.

"You can't resign," said Salazar.

"Why not?"

"Because you are the whole police department."

"I'm the sheriff," Ortega corrected him.

"You're the sheriff and the police too. No matter. I will not accept your resignation."

"That's right, I am everything," complained Ortega.

"What's the real problem?"

"I'm a one man show, just like Rambo!" said Ortega in anger. "I don't want to face the Air Force, the Army, the DEA, the CIA, and the KKK in this mess."

"There's no KKK in the valley," Salazar said.

"Someone burned a cross in my yard, god damn it!"

"It might have been Pachuco Pacheco," said Salazar. "He's been babbling about warding off evil spirits and demanding exorcisms. Listen to me. Let this matter run its own course. Just don't shoot anybody."

"What if they shoot me?"

"Nobody is gonna shoot the sheriff," Salazar said.

"The people aren't sending me any carrot cakes." Ortega said. "They are pulling guns out of cedar chests. Muerda, we

have more guns around here than opening day of elk season."
Ortega watched the Mayor rip his letter into tiny little pieces. "I can see," Salazar said with a smile, "that most of them are making money on this UFO. And the Governor promised this squabble will be resolved with everyone's feelings considered." Ortega leaned over and knocked on Salazar's desk. "Screw the Governor!" he shouted. This is High Noon and I don't want to be a Gary Cooper!"

CHAPTER THIRTY-TWO

DUKE
WHINED INSIDE
his doghouse. Something
was looking at him. When he
gathered the courage to stick his head
out, he heard swishing sounds in the night, like
ricocheting bullets. Unseen things zipped through the
darkness. They were on top of the barn and the house. They were on the porch. In fact, he sensed one on top of his dog house. Like a turtle, he slowly receded his head back into his sanctuary.

One zipped into Summer's room, traveling at cartoon speed. It latched itself onto the ceiling and then dropped down onto her bed to seemingly peer into her childish face. Summer's eyes opened and she screamed. The creature leaped back to the ceiling. Rachel and Joe rushed inside the bedroom and felt the intruder explode out of the room like a hot gush of wind.

"Mommy?" said Summer, hugging her teddy bear.

"Joe, I felt something leave the room." She went and picked up Summer.

"I didn't see it," said Joe.

"I felt it, Joe. Damn you. I've had enough. You're putting us in danger."

"Something looked at me, mommy."

"Summer will sleep with me until I figure out what to do," said Rachel.

She stopped at the door, "Joe, I love you, but . . .oh just go sleep with your flying saucer."

Joe Lucky did exactly as ordered.

He opened the locks and chains on the barn doors and gazed upon the UFO. It was a magnificent sleek machine, and a shiny oyster of hope and wonder. What kind of pearl was locked inside? Maybe it possessed a great gift of knowledge for the human race. But he knew, sooner or later, they would try to kill him to get it. Such was the cynical way of the world. Negativism in everything. In best selling books, in new philosophies, in new movements of human development; the human race was standing on a precipice and only contemplating the jump into darkness as the final pessimistic fate of humanity. He refused to stand on that side of the fence.

Why couldn't we develop a philosophy of hope and love, and teach our children these things. A child's wonder was beautiful and untouched. Why couldn't we go through life with that childish wonder where love was better than hate? Hope was better than despair. And still we couldn't see the plain truth before our eyes. It was so simple: all we needed to do is love. Joe Lucky rested on his cot until he closed his weary eyes and fell into a sound sleep.

Rachel opened the doors.

The morning rays seeped through the cracks of the barn. Joe's weird artworks gleamed in the sunlight between the rafters and every corner of the barn.

"Joe?" she called.

Joe Lucky stirred awake.

"Honey," answered Joe Lucky, "what's wrong?"

"I'm leaving, Joe. Dad is coming for Summer and me."

Joe Lucky leaped off the cot and rushed toward Rachel.

"It's not safe here," said Rachel. "Please don't try to argue. I made up my mind."

"Baby, don't do this, please."

A Ford Bronco came up the road and stopped in front of the barn. Sam Patterson climbed out and approached his daughter. "Everything talked out?" Sam asked Rachel. He was a thin man with curly white hair and kind blue eyes.

Rachel nodded.

"Hello, grandpa," Summer said.

"There's my girl," said Sam. He picked up Summer and spun her in a circle.

"Dad, why are you doing this?" Joe Lucky asked.

"I'm sorry, Joe." He put Summer down. "Things are running amok down here, scaring my daughter and granddaughter. It's not safe. And you don't know what's inside that thing in the barn. It could have a deadly virus that could wipe out mankind."

"Well, if it does," said Joe Lucky, "I must be a zombie because I'm still walking around." Joe Lucky's attempt at humor rang hollow.

Sam gathered up the suitcases. "You're a good man, Joe. But you were born with your brain inside your heart."

Joe Lucky hung his head. "Rachel," he said. "I love you. But I have to see this thing to the end. It's my journey, honey. Please try to understand."

Water came into Rachel's eyes. "I don't know what's happening."

Summer ran to Joe Lucky who went to his knees and kissed her on the forehead.

"Daddy, you OK?" she asked.

"I'm Ok, happy feet."

"Are you sure? If you're OK, we can come back." Summer started to cry. "I hope you find good in that space car."

"Me too," said Joe Lucky near tears.

"Summer get in the car," said Rachel. "Goodbye, Joe."

They boarded. Duke came out of his dog house and watched the Bronco bounce off. Summer waved from the back window. Sadly, Duke went back into his dog house. Joe Lucky went back into his barn and produced a full bottle of Jack Daniels from inside a loose plank on the barn wall.

He sat on the cot and got gloriously drunk.

In San Miguel, Sheriff Ortega looked out his office window and saw a wondrous sight. A flock of chickens were making a quick march for Pachuco Pacheco's truck. Ortega was so amazed that he went out to the front of the jail and watched the chickens waddle past his office. He chased a couple of wayward hens back into the pack by waving his hat.

It must be true, he thought, that God protects fools and drunks. It so happened that Pachuco, his poor friend, was in both of God's categories.

The chickens, including two red roosters, beat their
stubby wings to fly up onto the truck. A
couple of hearty hens flapped even
harder to roost on top of the
truck's cab. Pachuco came
out of his canvas tent
and shouted with
glorious
glee.

CHAPTER THIRTY-THREE

PETE DURAN, lead singer for the Hot Chili Peppers Band, stepped up to the microphone and crooned out the soul stirring "El Rancho Grande." He sang lustfully, lifting his sombrero into the air. The pool table had been pushed into a corner. A hundred boots pounded on the dance floor. Skirts whirled. Men howled like coyotes. Max Campos and Roberta Sandoval went skating from one side of the dance floor to the other. Julie One Owl helped Ducky deliver tray loads of tequila and beer. It was a festive dance.

Joe Lucky's truck raced into the parking lot and hit an elm tree. He rolled out of the truck and looked at the damage to his bumper. He whacked the truck with his baseball cap. He heard the song gush out of Ducky's Bar with its thumping beat.

Joe Lucky swayed beneath the waddling duck on the roof. He walked into Ducky's Bar and immediately eye-balled Max twirling Roberta in a circle. Pete Duran was taking the song home.

Joe Lucky picked up a beer bottle and hurled it. The bottle hit the great Mexican revolutionary Emile Zapata right in the nose, and ripped the portrait. A member of the band hit a wrong note on his guitar. Pete Duran petered out into a shrill ending. A few drum beats followed the guitars into a sour silence.

Joe Lucky called Max out.

"Hey, Max," yelled Joe Lucky. "You were a lousy football player and you're a lousy dancer! Got any salt peter to put into my beer, cabron?"

The crowd split in half.

Max smiled. "The only salt peter I would give to anybody," he said defiantly, "is Chili Mestas. He has twelve kids and one baking in the oven."

Max squared off. He took the stance of a gunfighter without the guns. His hands were curled at his hips. Joe Lucky swayed like a cobra. He took a deep breath and charged head-first.

"It was horrifying," Willie Garduno later told Sheriff Ortega. Max charged the same moment as Joe Lucky. And they bumped heads like mountain goats. Both recoiled and fell unconscious to the floor. Not one fist was launched. Not one boot connected. Not one curse was uttered. Just a sickening sound of hard head on hard head.

Max had a seizure on the floor and flopped around like a trout on the banks of the Conjeos River. Joe Lucky rose to his hands and knees, then hit the deck for a second time. The crowd enclosed the combatants. But it was a mission of rescue. Julie One Owl swore that Joe Lucky was snoring. Max still flopped until someone sat on his legs.

She had two men carry Joe Lucky to his truck and she drove him to his cot in the barn. Joe Lucky was up on the tractor the next morning, but Max Campos suffered migraine headaches for three days. It was said that Joe Lucky had the harder head of the two pendejos.

Perhaps the hardest head in San Miguel.

Down at Joe Lucky's Ranch, Jimmy Zoot was playing Texas Hold 'Um' with a group of UFO nuts. A pair of lanterns hung on poles and imbued light onto a folding card table. Moths fluttered around the lanterns beating their wings against the fluorescent light. The Beatles' "Lucy In The Sky With Diamonds" was blaring out of the speakers on top of the RV where Claire quietly gazed through the telescope into the night sky.

"The Beatles were great," said Jimmy.

Zack Smith, a nut, said, "remember when John Lennon said they were more popular than Jesus?" Zack puffed on a joint.

"Well they were not that great," replied Jimmy. "The Beatles never became a word in the dictionary."

"Are you sure?" asked Zack. "Seems they would be great enough for that."

"I raise you fifty cents," said a card player. He tossed two blue chips into the pile.

"I thought red was for quarters," complained Zack.

"White is for nickels," Jimmy explained toking on his joint, "red is for dimes and blue is for quarters. Jesus, man, can't you keep that straight?"

A red Jetta pulled up to the card players.

Tiny Tim climbed out of the car and rose to seven-foot-four inches in height. He weighed about three hundred pounds and had forearms like Popeye. His huge head was cropped short and that gave him a pair of elf ears. His blue eyes twinkled like those of a child.

Jimmy Zoot's roach nearly fell from his lips.

"Man, what a trip!" Jimmy exclaimed. "You're a big hombre. I hope you come in peace?"

"Is this the Joe Lucky ranch?" asked Tiny Tim.

"Did you have the dream too?" inquired Jimmy.

"No dream."

"Why did you come?"

"I saw Joe Lucky on the CBS News," said Tiny. "I quit my job and came here."

"How come?"

"I don't know."

"Do you have sleeping quarters," asked Jimmy.

"A tent."

"My name is Jimmy." You're here for a noble cause. We might be massacred by the military in the end but que sera, sera. You're here and so you're a believer."

"I'm Tiny Tim." The giant reached a huge hand into the Jetta and pulled out a canvas tent.

"I'll help you put up the tent," Jimmy said eagerly. "Hey Claire look at this giant!"

Claire waved from the top of the RV. She replied, "the Tewa Indians claim that the creator still lives in the mountains of San Miguel."

"Maybe he does?" said Jimmy. "And the point is?"

"The creator sometimes appears to the Tewa in the form of a

Sasquatch."

Jimmy went and stood by Tiny Tim. His head reached Tiny Tim's belt buckle. He looked up. He didn't see any creator clues in the colossus. Claire climbed back on top of the RV, and did a dance. She shouted: "There comes one! Jimmy, I see one!"

Her excited cries caused a stir in the conglomeration of UFO people. They exited RVs and campers and vans. They rushed to their own telescopes. Tiny Tim and Jimmy walked toward the entrance gate to have a look. They watched a pair of lights approach in the dark. They bobbed a great distance. Everyone held their breath. And then they approached on the road.

Tiny Tim asked, "Is it a flying saucer?"

"Sure is something," said Jimmy.

They waited in anticipation. They heard a puttering noise and saw the two lights of Joe Lucky's tractor pull up to his mail box on the gate.

"Mister, are you Joe Lucky?" asked Tiny Tim.

Joe Lucky stepped down off the tractor and removed his mail from the box. He sorted through envelopes.

"Any good news, Joe?" asked Jimmy.

"Bills," said Joe Lucky. He climbed back onto the tractor and looked at Tiny Tim. "Jesus, how tall are you?" he asked. "Seven-foot-four." "Well, you ought to be playing basketball. Why don't you people go home!" Claire pointed the flashlight on Joe Lucky. "We're here for you, Joe," she said, "and your mission for God." "I'm on no mission," answered Joe Lucky. "Hell, I don't even have a game plan. I'm making things up on the run." Joe Lucky put the tractor in gear and puttered home.

CHAPTER THIRTY-FOUR

PACHUCO
ROSE WITH THE
crowing of his roosters.
He neatly folded his canvas
cover and munched on some of
Julie One Owl's tacos. Wearing a straw
hat for the hot sun, he sat in the back of the
truck and carved into a block of cottonwood. Pachuco had
quickly learned that the gringos were eager to pay more money
for his crude santos, the almost half-finished pieces.
Occasionally, he dipped his hand into a sack of chicken feed
and sowed a sea of white chickens on the street. The chickens
pecked rapidly for seed, and each managed to keep one eye on
their master.

Tourists were already milling outside Tita's Bed and
Breakfast drinking coffee and looking at her green jalepeno
plants. Up on the second floor, CIA Bill inspected his 9 m.m.
Beretta with the orange tip of a Russian silencer. He cocked the
breach with an ominous click. On the bed, he had a .22
derringer with a belt buckle carrier. He snapped the tiny
derringer into the exact cut-out shape in the buckle.

"Option 3," he said to motivate himself, "take the Cadillac."

CIA Bill heard a commotion on the street. He went to the
window and saw a big Peterbilt big rig scatter Pachuco's
chickens into a frenzy. On the side, emblazoned in black letters:

CNN NEWS.

"Kiss me Beth," he uttered.

A TV truck was big news in San Miguel. Some of the citizens
leaped in their cars and followed the truck to Joe Lucky's ranch.
They watched it stop in the meadow. Bill Clauson, news
correspondent, looked out at the growing mass of people at the
gate and said, "Dale, get some back story shots of these wackos."

"What kind of shots?" asked Dale. He looked at the odd assortment. "Do I need to be worried here?"

"I don't see any guns," said Clauson. Dale gathered his gear and walked into the crowd for footage. Clauson laughed and joked with Cliff, his driver, a likeable blond man from New York.

"He might get clubbed to death in there," said Clauson. "Then, my man, we'll have a hell of a story."

Cliff laughed too. Clauson was handsome and nailed down the female numbers for the network. He was charming from his white teeth to his Oxford loafers. His sandy hair was neatly combed, every hair frozen in place by 3XXX hairspray. His blue eyes hinted of mirth. His popularity was growing so fast at CNN that someone up the ladder hinted of a possible anchor job on the coveted evening news.

There was a lot of squawking inside the camp. Dale came running, the camera bobbing on his shoulder. He dived into the Peterbilt cab, shouting, "Go! Go! Go!"

Cliff was startled and stripped the gears before heading down the road for the ranch.

"What happened?" asked Clauson.

"You're not going to believe me."

"I'm on a job assignment to interview a redneck who found a UFO in his pasture, for god's sake. I'll believe anything."

"There was a giant in there," Dale said. "Biggest lout I ever saw in my life!"

"And?"

"He said if I pull the trigger on my camera he would pop my head like a pimple."

Dale calmed himself with a cigarette. "This is worse than Afghanistan," he said.

In the kitchen, Joe Lucky removed a chicken fried steak dinner from the microwave. He sat at his kitchen table. He was miserable. He missed the singing of Summer and the sounds of Rachel tinkering in the kitchen. He missed the smell of Rachel. He missed her beef stroganoff and Sunday spaghetti dinners. He missed the warmth of her body at night in bed. He missed his mouth with an unsightly glob of his TV dinner.

He tossed the dinner into the trash.

Joe Lucky walked to the barn and moped on his cot. He looked up at his sculptures dangling in the sunlight, and for the first time admitted they were pieces of crap. He looked at Snippy and thought she was a worthless bag of bones. He glared at the UFO and said, "you're probably worthless too. You're probably not even alien. If you opened up I bet Chinese people would walk out holding chop sticks."

Joe Lucky fetched his jack hummer and fired up his compressor. He climbed up the ladder to the UFO. Finding good footing on the ring, he jack-hammered into the UFO with the sound of a 50-caliber machine gun. He hammered so hard his teeth hurt. Finally, to his utter amazement, a small piece broke off the craft. Joe Lucky picked up the piece and studied the strange metal in his palm. He almost expected it to chirp. Suddenly, the metal liquefied and was sucked back into the same position on the UFO.

"Wow," exclaimed Joe Lucky, "who are you guys?"

Outside, the Peterbilt pulled up to the barn.

Clauson climbed down and pounded on the barn doors. Dale and Cliff opened the door on the trailer and started unloading equipment into the yard. Clauson went back to the Peterbilt and honked the air horn and frightened the irascible Texas doves from the tree in the yard.

Joe Lucky came out of the barn and pulled off his gloves. He was not amused by CNN. Clauson approached with a Colgate smile.

"You doing some farming down yonder?" asked Clauson in his best redneck rendition.

"Yonder where?" answered Joe.

Clauson smiled and pointed to the meadow.

"Can't farm over there," said Joe. "It's booby trapped."

"Oh," said Clauson.

Joe Lucky removed his baseball cap and wiped his brow with his shirt. "What can I do for you?"

"Mr. Lucky, I'm Bill Clauson with CNN and I want to do an

interview."

"I saw you on TV," said Joe Lucky. "I suppose you would like to see it?"

"See it?"

"You know." Joe Lucky winked at Clauson.

"So you do have one?"

"You ain't a spy for the government?"

"Hell no," said Clauson. "I secretly agree with you disgruntled ranchers. Hell, you can blow up anything you want." He smiled. "But if it's the CNN building, let me know in advance."

"Shit, if anything gets blown up," said Joe Lucky, "it will be me."

He jumped off the tractor and opened the locks on the barn doors. He swung the double doors open. Clauson walked into the barn, mouth agape. Dale and Cliff dropped boxes on the ground and approached in awe.

"This is a hoax, right?" said Clauson.

"I didn't build it," said Joe Lucky. "I can barely repair my lawn mower."

"It came from outer space?" asked Dale.

"It came from somewhere," said Joe Lucky.

"You will be the most famous man in the world," uttered Clauson.

"Maybe," said Dale, "he'll be famous in five hundred years when the thing is declassified."

"How can they deny it's existence if we film it, boys?" said Clauson.

"They'll kill all of us, that's how," said Cliff. "I don't want to die in a Colorado barn!"

They approached the UFO.

"Cliff, you been watching too much X-Files," said Clauson. He put his hand lovingly on the flying saucer.

"Let's set up for dramatics, boys. I want a huge American flag hanging from the rafters and covering the flying saucer. At the right moment, we'll expose it to the world. Walter Cronkite, slide a cheek! Here I come!" shouted Clauson.

At that moment, Misty-2 was propelled into a new orbit from the coast of Africa to North America by seven metric tons of rocket fuel. Misty-- the billion dollar spy in the sky satellite — unfolded its complex super-sensitive panels as it twirled in the weightlessness of space. Misty focused and clicked on images of Joe Lucky and Clauson in the yard.

Down at NORAD, Snoopy Taylor could see such precise details that he determined Clauson had a Parker pen in his shirt pocket and a Budweiser in his hand. Much to his chagrin, Misty-2 couldn't see inside the barn. Blue tracking screens displayed various images of the ranch. One image focused right onto the black snout of Duke, his long, brown head extended out of the doghouse.

"Jack, I want you to go down there and sit in on this Clauson bullshit. You will represent the military point of view."

"And what view is that?" asked Captain Jack.

"The military's policy is to always deny everything. You should know that. And have intelligence hook up one of those tiny cameras on your hat. I want a close look at this thing. You never know what this mad cowboy is going to do! God damn, I hope he doesn't show it on National TV!" "And if he does, sir, what do I say?"

"Say it's a fraud," said Snoopy Taylor. "Nobody has ever seen a flying saucer! So who's going to know what is real or fake."

CHAPTER THIRTY-FIVE

"DUCKY, I'M BUYING the house a round," said Julie One Owl. The bar was booming with customers. There were tourists, UFO nuts, citizens of neighboring counties, and even a busload of bible thumpers from Denver. Ducky rushed from table to table with a tray of beers. He returned to the bar and wiped his brow with his apron.

"Aye, I need a cocktail girl," he exclaimed. He went down the bar pouring shots of tequila. "Anybody shoot that gabacho Joe Lucky yet?" he asked.

"I hope not," said Taco Sanchez. "I'm selling the heck out of my potatoes at my stand."

Julie One Owl inspected her tequila in the light and then downed it. "I got a lot of gringos in my café."

"I heard that crybaby Thomas is frying more burgers than McDonalds," said Taco.

"He's finally earning his money," Julie One Owl said. "He's the only unhappy person in San Miguel."

"Is it true Joe Lucky lost his wife?" asked Ducky.

"She left," said Julie One Owl. "There was some spooky stuff going down at the ranch. So she ran away to Denver and took the little girl."

"Did she go with another man?" asked Taco hopefully.

"No, pendejo," said Julie One Owl. "She left with her father. When I drove Joe home after the brawl with Max, he woke up holding his head in the barn and said to me: 'Did we have sex?'"

"Well?" inquired Ducky.

"How dare you!" hissed Julie One Owl. "I won't have a one night stand with a drunken lout!"

"Not that," said Ducky. "Did you see it?"

Julie One Owl said, "it's beautiful. It stirred me to the soul. In a strange way, it was almost a religious thing."

They drank in silence. Then Taco thought of something. "Where's Max?" "I heard he was giving fishing lessons on the Conejos," someone said. "Fishing lessons, my ass," said Julie One Owl. "He's guarding his mary jane by gunpoint." "This is true," said Ducky. "I'm afraid to go fishing because I might step on a damn land mine." "Aye," said Julie One Owl, "then, mi amigo, your stubby leg would be as puny as your pecker."

CHAPTER THIRTY-SIX

SLOWLY,
BRIGHT STUDIO
lights came up inside
Joe Lucky's barn. Clauson
sat supremely behind a desk. Joe
Lucky sat to his left with his goggles
on top of his baseball cap. Captain Jack, spiffy
in his Air Force dress blues, sat to the right. Dale
manned the camera and Cliff was the prop man. He stood
by a huge American flag that hung in the background to conceal
the UFO. Clauson was at his impeccable best in shirt and tie. He
gazed with his blue eyes into the camera.

"Are we going live. . .?" he asked Dale.

Dale gave him a salute.

"Tonight, duty has summoned me to a ranch in Colorado. A place where the West was really won. A place where people love the land. I was compelled to leave the studio for this musty barn in Colorado to hopefully look upon a wondrous thing. A flying saucer! And interview the man who found it in his meadow. Mr. Joe Lucky."

Joe Lucky smiled.

"We have space intruders in this barn," said Clauson. "And they may have come from beyond the Pluto moons. Are they friend or foe? Only Joe Lucky may know the answer."

"I think they are friendly," said Joe Lucky.

"Joe, how did you become public enemy number one?" asked Clauson.

"One night I looked out of my bedroom window and saw a flying saucer crash into my meadow. Now, everybody wants it."

"Indeed," said Clauson, "do you mean the government and this gentleman to my right, Captain Jack Holloway?"

Captain Jack squirmed in his chair.

"He's one of them," said Joe Lucky. "The Air Force. The Army. And somebody with an Uncle Sam up his family tree. I even had a call from that lunatic in Iran. He wants it, too."

"You mean Iranian President Mahmoud Ahmadinejad?" asked Clauson in astonishment.

"Yeah, that prickhead," said Joe Lucky.

"Is it true the government offered you a million bucks for the flying saucer?" asked Clauson.

"Yeah, it was the shady plumber with an uncle named Sam."

"I just want to say this is a noble stand," said Clauson, "since Joe Lucky is losing his ranch to bank scamps."

Captain Jack interceded. "We believe Mr. Lucky conjured up this hoax to raise funds to pay off his debts."

Down in the camp, Jimmy, Claire and Tiny Tim munched on a pizza from Pizza Hut.

"The bastards can't kill him now," said Jimmy.

"Joe is on a saintly course," said Claire. "And you know the fate of saints."

Tiny Tim sipped on a beer and watched intensely. The TV displayed the FOR SALE signs nailed to the porch. The house looked dark and lonely.

Clauson looked directly into the camera.

"Joe Lucky has lost his wife and child," said Clauson, "due to his stubborn endeavor to harbor this flying saucer in his barn. And even his dog, Duke, is suffering from severe depression and symptoms of PTSD. The poor creature is in need of Prozac."

The TV displayed Duke's dog house, equally dark and sad. Dale looked at the monitor and gave Clauson the 'thumbs up' sign. This was some awesome stuff, Dale thought.

"And still the man turned down a million bucks," continued Clauson. "Is this integrity or stupidity? Either way, you have to admire Joe Lucky."

At NORAD, Snoopy Taylor puffed on a large cigar. He watched a giant monitor and paced nervously.

"This Clauson is a subversive red. I ought to send a Navy Seal team down there and castrate the bastard. That would really give a shrill voice to his shows!"

On the monitor, the TV image shifted to Captain Jack.

"We invited General Snoopy Taylor to appear on our program," said Clauson. "He refused and send his underling, Jack Holloway. Jack, how does the Air Force deal with the presence of UFO's?"

Captain Jack said, "the Air Force has never found any plausible explanations for UFO sightings. There were 97 sightings here in the San Miguel Valley last year. Not one has been established as fact."

On cue, Cliff pulled on a rope to lift the huge American flag and exposed the shiny UFO.

"What is that, sir?" Clauson asked Captain Jack.

"That's a forgery. A get rich scheme."

"Joe," said Clauson, "will you give us a short demonstration as to the theory of a real UFO."

Joe Lucky, Clauson and Captain Jack approached the UFO. Joe fired up his torch, pulled down his goggles, and applied the blue flame to the belly of the UFO. Sparks bounced everywhere. Suddenly, Joe Lucky seized Captain Jack's hand and applied it to the surface of the UFO.

Captain Jack looked like a sheep facing the shears. "How dare you!" he protested.

"As we can see," said Clauson with a toothy smile, "the metal is foreign. It's cool as a cucumber. This is too elaborate for a hoax. I declare this as alien metal!"

Joe Lucky smiled at the camera, still wearing his goggles.

Snoopy Taylor nearly lost his wits. He pounded a massive fist onto a desk. Personnel sat frozen in their chairs.

"Magnify the UFO!" he demanded.

A frightened communication specialist clicked the UFO to full screen.

"What a beautiful baby!" ranted Snoopy Taylor. We could leap-frog two centuries with that technology. Hell, I could find Jimmy Hoffa and give him a colostomy from deep space! Now somebody tell me! What is my flying saucer doing in that redneck's barn?"

In the Denver suburb, Summer watched her daddy smiling into the TV camera.

"Mommy, come here!"

Rachel came in from the kitchen wiping her hands on her apron.

"Mommy, look at daddy on TV," said Summer.

Rachel sat on the sofa. "Daddy made the news," she said, hugging her daughter.

Inside the barn, Clauson, Captain Jack and Joe Lucky returned to the table.

"Joe," said Clauson, "I must, as a journalist, probe on the negative side. What if that machine has the makings of another 'Invasion of the Body Snatchers' germinating in its belly?"

"The problem with the modern world is that we look at the dark things and avoid the light," said Joe Lucky. "I have to believe there is good inside of it. I have to believe I'm on the right path. How can you exist without faith?"

Clauson chuckled. "It did slice your milk cow in half."

"I think it was a matter of research," Joe Lucky retorted. "We do the same thing. We send apes into space and we shoot cancer cells in animals. We subject animals to every despicable experiment in the book. We call it a noble thing like science. Maybe these creatures have their own scientific method?"

"Good point," Clauson agreed.

Down at Ducky's Bar, the citizenry were absorbed in the broadcast on Ducky's television.

"Shit, we're famous," said Ducky.

"No, Joe Lucky is famous," said Julie One Owl lifting a shot to his image on the TV.

"Viva, Joe Lucky!" they shouted.

They hoisted shots of tequila to honor him.

Inside Joe Lucky's barn, the American flag went back up as a background.

"Joe Lucky," asked Clauson, "would you like to say anything else?"

"Yes, I would," answered Joe Lucky. "Why must we hate and launch wars? Mankind has a dismal record of warfare, massacres and profound animosity. We learned to wage wars and launch torpedoes under the deepest oceans. We learned to wage wars in our skies. The next step is to wage wars in space, and carry our animosities to other dimensions. I don't want to inherit this legacy as a human being. Maybe this UFO was a warning to us? And that's why I can't sell it. It may be our only salvation."

Clauson felt a tear come to his eye. His voice broke with emotion. "How eloquent this man has spoken. A wisdom beyond his education." He paused to regain his emotions. "Captain Jack, maybe you have the answer?"

"Well, Mr. Clauson, there are haters in the world, and it's our job to exterminate the haters. Then, maybe we can build a better world."

"In closing," said Clauson, "I would like to ask Joe Lucky what would happen if you gave them the UFO?"

"If I give them the UFO," said Joe Lucky, "they will just pry it open, and dissect them like frogs in a lab."

Clauson concluded with a dramatic flourish:

"There you have it from a barn in Colorado. The greatest story since a child was born in a stable under a blazing star. I believe we have discovered a true messenger of peace. He's Joe Lucky and he can be mentioned in the same breath with Gandhi and Martin L. King. I just hope he has a better fate than those gentlemen."

Dale focused a close-up on Clauson's pretty baby blues.

"We say good-night for CNN with these great words:

"The more helpless a creature, the more it deserves to be protected by man from man."

Outside, LRRP's moved rapidly through the meadow. Sgt. Reemes made a hand signal. The LRRP's went down into a shooting stance and M16's barked loudly. The antennas on top of the CNN trailer snapped off in the volley of bullets. Another volley and a couple of tires hissed flat. As quickly as they came, the LRRP's receded back into the meadow and sank down into their foxholes. Inside the barn, Dale hit the deck. "I knew they would kill us," he shouted. The lights went dead. The monitor blinked out. "Are we still live?" asked a calm Clauson at the desk.

"No, we're not live!" yelled Dale. "And we're going to
be as dead as our juice too!" Cliff was pale.
He quipped, "that was riveting, I must
say. "I bet the ratings are off
the charts," mused
a delighted
Clauson."

CHAPTER THIRTY-SEVEN

A
MATCH
flickered in the
dark and ignited the wick
of a candle. Sheriff Ortega was
on his knees before the blessed Virgin
de Guadalupe. Her benign face looked kindly
down at him. "Holy Madre," said Ortega, "protect
our town and our people. Protect me from becoming road kill. Amen."

He left the church, cap in hand, and stopped at Pachuco's truck. Chickens stood guard on the truck in the light of a full moon. They cast one evil eye on Ortega.

"Hey Pachuco," Ortega said.

Pachuco stuck his head out of the canvas tent. "Hola, Sheriff," he said.

"Why don't you go home?"

"I won't. Not until Padre Gomez does an exorcism and spreads holy water in my house."

Down the street, Julie One Owl approached with a plate of tacos and burritos.

"Here she comes, Miss America," Ortega said with sarcasm. "I hear business is booming at the cafe, que no?"

"So shoot me," Julie One Owl said. "I'm a capitalist. You are right. This is America. I hope you don't do nothing stupid to mess this up." She gave the plate to Pachuco who swallowed down a bean burrito.

"It's messed up already," retorted Ortega.

Thomas came running down the street, waving his apron like a white flag. "Julie!" Es un milagro! Come quick!"

"What's he babbling about?" asked Ortega.

"Is the cafe on fire?" asked Julie One Owl.

"No. Rosa was making tortillas and we have a miracle!" said Thomas, his face full of joy. He pulled Julie One Owl up the street.

"Behold," Ortega told Pachuco, "La Luna is full."

Ortega walked toward the cafe in wide strides. He checked his hip for his big pistol. Miracles these days seemed to require firepower. Pachuco gave chase. His flock of chickens leaped off the truck and followed, clucking loudly.

Max's lot was full of automobiles. Even at this late hour, the cafe was bustling with diners. Ortega walked into a bee hive. Tables were full of tourists. Some of the UFO nuts were munching Julie's UFO burgers, and nibbling painfully on fresh green jalepenos.

Ortega went into the kitchen. Pachuco and his flock followed. The chickens pecked around for crumbs. Rosa, a heavy woman with white hair, was very emotional.

"Dios mio!" she uttered.

Rosa cupped her hands in prayer. Stacks of tortillas were piled in mounds on the prepping table.

"Que pasa?" asked Pachuco, wide-eyed.

"Pachuco!" yelled Julie One Owl. "Get them chickens out of my kitchen! Do you want the health department to close down my cafe?"

Pachuco was shamed by the insult. He spoke to his chickens like children:

"Come on lovely ones. We're not welcome. Let's go." He led the chicken procession out of the kitchen.

"Has everybody lost their minds?" asked Ortega.

"There is always a skeptic among the faithful," muttered Rosa. "Look here." She picked up a tortilla. "See, it has a flying saucer, and above is the face of the blessed Virgin Mary!"

Truly, the milagro tortilla's burn pattern was shaped like a UFO with the Saturn ring. But the amazing thing was the lovely face of the Virgin Mary hovering above the UFO.

Ortega took a closer look. It was an exquisite rendition. The Holy Mother had a Mona Lisa smile. Ortega faltered for words. "This is a blessing!" said Julie One Owl. "Thank God for Joe Lucky. San Miguel will prosper in our blessed Mother's good graces. It's San Miguel's own Holy Tortilla!"

CHAPTER THIRTY-EIGHT

GIANT
BUBBLES
floated upward.
Joe Lucky sat on his
tractor seat and blew bubbles
through Summer's bubble blower. He was
bored and had parked the tractor in front of the
double barn doors as another obstacle to scoundrels.

A lightning bolt ripped the dark sky in half. Drops of rain fell onto Joe Lucky. He scampered under the tractor and entered the barn through a crawl space he had cut at the bottom of a door.

He sat on the cot and clicked on the radio:

"Rain, rain go away," said the same sultry radio voice, "come back another day. Hello out there to Joe Lucky, our new folk hero. Joe, buddy, you have become a true enemy of the state. Your story is a folk tale of the first rank. Our government has ordered some shady characters into the San Miguel valley because they have some. . ."

"Lying Eyes'" by the Eagles filtered out of the radio.

Joe Lucky rested morosely on the cot, listening to the sad lyrics and missing Rachel so much that his heart hurt. The radio voice interrupted the lyrics:

"Don't despair Joe Lucky. It is always darkest before the dawn."

He listened to the rhythmical rain drip from the patched hole in the roof and plink down onto the slumbering UFO.

Suddenly, the barn glowed brightly with yellow, orange and blue colors. Snippy twirled in the rafters in a clattering of bones. The sculptures banged into one another like hammer blows.

Joe Lucky sat upright. Each raindrop made the UFO pulsate
with colorful lights. The hues glowed on his
face. The rain, he thought in exaltation.
The song on the radio disintegrated into

static and the microwave oven dinged
repeatedly. Joe Lucky shivered
on the cot. Then the top of
the UFO opened like
an eyelid. And
they finally
emerged.

CHAPTER THIRTY-NINE

ACROSS
HIGHWAY 160,
a carnival had sprouted
overnight on the prairie. Grubby
workers scrambled to set up electrical lines
and gas generators. A towering ferris wheel and
handsome carousel had already been assembled. There
was a tent for a freak show with lurid posters of a fat woman, a two-headed goat, a naked beauty with a beard and the smallest weight-lifter in the world: a poster of a midget holding baby barbells. Workers had set up a hot dog and hamburger stand, which also advertised cotton candy and sodas. One worker filled alien-faced balloons with an air compressor.

And in the middle of this frenzy, showman Billy Batty, a sixty year old, smooth-talking crook with a pot belly and cheap suit, shouted orders through a megaphone.

"Step it up! You know the routine! You, Flavio, check the gas in the generators!"

Billy Batty walked back toward his trailer with

"BILLY BATTY'S CARNIVAL SHOW"

on the side in bold black letters. Generators coughed to life and the whole show took on a magical light. Cheap carnival music floated out into the dark. Billy Batty shouted into his megaphone:

"Come one, come all! Come see the famous Billy Batty Carnival Show!"

The Zoots, Tiny Tim and a pack of unruly children stood in awe at the side of Highway 160.

"What's the admission price?" asked Jimmy.

"One lousy dollar my friend," said Billy Batty.

"Why did you bring a carnival here, mister?" asked Claire. "We're on a spiritual mission."

Jimmy elbowed her in the side in protest. Billy Batty approached and stood directly in the middle of the highway.

"So am I, dear," he said. "Say, who is that big boy?" Billy Batty crossed the highway to look up at Tiny Tim. "How tall are you?" he asked.

"Why."

"I might have a position for you."

"Doing what?"

"Doing nuthin'. How tall are you?"

"Seven-foot-four."

Billy Batty circled him, pondering deeply. "Yes, I see it! Come see the tallest man in the world!"

Tiny Tim placed a giant paw on Billy Batty's shoulder to still him. "I'm not the tallest man in the world. There's a Russian who is seven-foot-eight."

Billy Batty removed the paw and circled again. "Hell, boy, them's facts. Americans don't give a shit about facts. They demand the meat in the nut. The thrill of wonder. We'll put some lifters on your shoes and presto! You're the tallest man in the world!"

"That's fudgin'," Tiny Tim said, looking down at this nervous nit. He started back for the camp. Billy Batty shouted:

"Looky there! What has America come to? You give a boy a
  chance for travel and adventure and fame and what does
    he say: 'it's fudgin'." Jimmy and Claire and the UFO
      nuts and their children returned back to the
        camp and took up chores. Billy Batty
         still had enthusiasm. He shouted
          into his megaphone: "Now,
           where is this fellow
            who found a
             real flying
              saucer?"

CHAPTER FORTY

A
FULL
moon dangled
in the night like a
ballroom globe. Frogs croaked
from the grassy banks of the Conejos
River, and occasionally there was a splash of a
frog taking a dip. Sheriff Ortega's Dodge Ram was
parked on the bridge. Ortega turned on his flashing red
lights and Max stepped out of the willows, swatting at
mosquitoes. "Hola, Max," said Ortega, "what did you want to
show me?"

"Come here," said Max. "Bring your flashlight."

Max walked beneath the bridge and Ortega followed.

"Look there," said Max.

Ortega pointed his flashlight. There were hundreds of bats hanging upside down. Ortega shined the light on Max's face.

"They're just bats," he said.

"Not just bats," explained Max. "Those are Mexican bats and they shouldn't be here. They go as far as Austin, Texas to breed. After they do the dirty deed, they fly back to Mexico."

"So?"

"Like the Texas Doves, they don't want to go home."

"So?"

"Something is screwing up their sonar," said Max. 'I think that's why they don't fly home."

"Listen Max," said Ortega, "when is the mota ready to harvest? You know, I turn my head sometimes. I like a jolt of mota once in a blue moon. I know times are hard, amigo. Besides, how you going to sell your used tires when my Trojan rubbers have more tread? There are government spooks running around down here. As much as you dislike me, I still don't want to see you tossed into a Federal prison. Don't plant mota after

this harvest. Are we good?" Max walked off,
looking over his shoulder like a guilty cat.
Ortega heard Max's voice float out of the
willows: "What about the bats?" Ortega
took another look at the hanging bats
They stared at him with beady
eyes. "Nothing to do," he
said. "I can't deport bats
on a bus. I guess We'll
all die from the
pinche bird
flu."

CHAPTER FORTY-ONE

JOE
LUCKY
looked upon
some beautiful beings.
They were almost translucent
and four feet tall. They had feminine
faces with lovely, black deer eyes. The heads
were oval and hairless and they lifted three fingers
to probe into the alien air. The leader, exquisitely beautiful,
wore a telepathic, silver head band. They zipped through great
gaps of space and crawled on the roof and walls like insects. But
it was the water that had seemingly awakened the creatures.
They caught drops of water in their hands and licked joyfully.
The creatures spoke in droning sounds, like grasshoppers in the
hot sun.

All looked at Joe Lucky who sat dumbfounded on his
cot. The creatures rejoiced on the walls and roof,
darting from one place to another. The leader
made a great leap from a roof rafter to land
on all fours in front of Joe Lucky. The
creature droned and looked directly
into his face. "Hi," he said.
"I'm Joe Lucky. Welcome
to earth. Please
don't kill
me."

CHAPTER FORTY-TWO

SAN
MIGUEL
continued to
prosper. Pachuco was
selling Santos as quickly as
he could whittle them. He was gaining
a reputation as one of the great Hispanic
artists in the American Southwest. He received
a letter from a Taos, New Mexico gallery who wanted
to represent his work. The church was also raking in the cash. Tourists and religious fanatics were packing the church to gaze upon the Holy Tortilla which was placed in a glass case in front of the altar. And then the Virgin de Guadalupe started to cry blood. This really did the trick. People came from all over the Southwest to light candles (fifty cents apiece) and whisper "Hail Marys" to honor both of the miracles. Padre Gomez was basking in the new Catholic spotlight. Not to mention, his coffers were overflowing. Shop owners sold their parking spaces for ten dollars an hour and were quite content to skim off the miracles. As one crowd exited the church, Padre Gomez quickly hustled in the next one.

Somebody rang a joyous bell in the belfry. The street was clogged with traffic. Horns honked. Agitated dogs barked, racing along and snapping at passing tires. The Native Americans were quietly in the money, hawking turquoise jewelry and trinkets. After all the injustices and crimes perpetrated against the Native American, not to mention stealing all their lands, they had revenge by hawking cheap dreamcatchers and other tokens to the eager tourists. An elderly grandmother sold fried bread and applied honey from a squirt bottle for five bucks apiece.

Down at the cafe, Julie One Owl watched the famous Denver muralist, Carlota Espinoza, paint a mural in her striking style on the cafe's wall. The Holy Tortilla radiated from the center. Above the tortilla, the beautiful face of the Virgin hovered in a heavenly and starry sky. All around the Holy Tortilla was the epic story of Joe Lucky and the UFO. He was portrayed as a loner, dragging the UFO across the meadow while surrounded by Army tanks. Flying jets and drones flew over his head. And the UFO nuts were presented in a crowd image at a fence, moon faces beaming with hope.

"I should have never let go of the Holy Tortilla," lamented Julie One Owl.

"Mija, it's a good thing for the church," said Carlota. "It's converting more people than John The Baptist."

"I wouldn't be surprised if someone nominates Joe Lucky for sainthood," said Julie One Owl.

"I think somebody did," Carlota said. "Emma Lopez wrote to the Vatican and Bishop Tayofa."

Julie One Owl snorted at the thought of Joe Lucky as a saint. She looked at Max's downtrodden repair shop. He had set up a stand of his own advertising:

PINON NUTS FOR SALE.

Hippies approached his stand.

"Hey, man," said a hippie, "they say you got some mean grass. Dino sent me."

Max reached under the booth and produced a ziplock plastic bag. "Fifty bucks," he said. "It's freshly cut and a good high."

"Man, how good? The price is high too," complained the hippie. He collected money from the group. More hippies wandered over to the stand.

"It's so good, mi amigo," said Max, "you'll be seeing hundreds of UFO's."

Julie One Owl entered the madness inside her cafe. Waitresses rushed among the tables delivering fancy plates of food and picking up dirty dishes. The Zoots and Tiny Tim were seated at a table. Children pointed at the colossus. Julie One Owl approached their table.

"Aren't you the leader of the UFO people?" she asked Jimmy.

"I was the first to come," explained Jimmy. "But nobody has

called me the leader."

"We came on a religious mission," explained Claire. "Joe Lucky is a holy man."

"Yiiii," cried Julie One Owl, "do all of you hope to catch a flight on a UFO with Joe to visit God?"

"Do you believe in aliens?" asked Claire.

"No, tu es loca?"

"Do you believe in God?"

"Yes, of course," said Julie One Owl.

"Have you ever seen Him?" asked Claire.

"No," said Julie One Owl.

"Well, there you go," Claire said with satisfaction. "I've never seen God or an alien. I just believe in both."

Julie One Owl walked off, pondering Claire's new enlightenment.

A little girl tugged on Jimmy's arm. "Mister, did the UFO bring the giant down to earth?

"No, honey," said Jimmy, "Tiny is from Texas."

Tiny Tim patted the little girl on the head with one huge paw.

In the kitchen, Tomas slapped burgers on the hot grill and cursed in Spanish. He dipped curly fries into hot sizzling grease. Rosa was forming balls of dough and rolling them into flat oval patterns on the prepping table. She stamped the dough with an iron tool to mark an imprint of a UFO.

"We need a bigger kitchen," complained Rosa, sprinkling flour on the flattened dough.

Thomas was exasperated. "We need a dishwasher and a prep cook."

"What is this," said Julie One Owl, "the Ramada Inn?"

In his kitchen Joe Lucky packed groceries into a box. The kitchen missed Rachel. Dirty dishes were piled everywhere. The trash can overflowed with empty TV dinners. He went into the bedroom and looked in the closet for Rachel's styrofoam head. He removed a black bushy wig, and then placed the head on the pillow of the bed. He used other pillows to shape a human form under the blankets. Contemplating, he removed his John Deere baseball cap and placed it on top of the styrofoam head so that the brim peeped out of the blankets. Joe Lucky removed three boxes of 30-ought-six bullets from a dresser. He went into the living room and clicked on the television. As he loaded his rifle, he watched a journalist standing before the entrance to NORAD:

"Joe Lucky, claimed one military spokesman at the secret NORAD base, is at war with our government because he is losing his ranch due to his own malfeasance. And the government will not provoke the rancher and make him into some sort of folk hero. They are searching for other solutions to the problem."

Joe Lucky sank back into his recliner, lifting the rifle to test the sights.

"Meanwhile, the San Miguel Valley is flourishing with tourists and UFO cults from as far away as Germany."

A new television shot showed Main Street of San Miguel, full of activities and people. Children ran amok, fists clenched full of firecrackers. A flying saucer spun in the middle of the street, propelled by human legs, and gushes of sparks emerged from the cardboard box head. "As one local woman put it," the journalist said as he looked squarely into the camera, "Mr. Joe Lucky is even more prosperous than the 'Pikes Peak Or Bust' gold strike of 1859."

CHAPTER FORTY-THREE

A
MAN
dressed in
black sat before
a smoky fire in a cave
in Petroglyph Canyon. He had
been in the cave for a spell. The bare
essentials for life were scattered about the
gloomy cave: a jug of water, cans of food, a wool
blanket and other bleak implements of a hermit. A

"REPENT" sign rested against the cave wall. He muttered verses from a tattered bible on his lap. Prehistoric petroglyphs glowed on the wall from the light of the fire. There were clumsy representations of antelope, bear, birds and bison. There were numerous renditions of the sun to indicate by their sheer number that these ancient people revered a sun god.

There was also a strange drawing.

An image that looked amazingly like a UFO and it was descending out of a sun, forever spiraling down to earth through the centuries. The man in black focused on this image. He could hear the ancient spirits and could feel them soaring inside the cave like gushes of cold wind.

The man in black knew that the San Miguel valley was seeped in this ancient history and renowned for the prehistoric art that predated Columbus by a thousand years. He had discovered this cave as a young student in archaeology. And the remoteness of the valley and the canyons was the very survival of these long-lost artists. The images had endured, untouched by human defacing. In the evening and morning light, the petroglyphs were a wonder and a marvel to gaze upon. If anything, they symbolized the mysticism of the whole valley and the art spoke to him as a driving force in his own quest for salvation.

Like Jesus, he went off into the famous "Great Sand Dunes"

which nearly killed Don Diego de Vargas long ago, and had his own vision quest.

He must announce the coming Rapture. He placed his quivering hand upon an ancient hand print on the wall. He seemed to draw power from this ritual. His eyes glazed over and his face became bright. He turned and walked out of the cave and climbed up the rim of a canyon. Below, he could see the enchanting lights of the carnival on the vast prairie. It looked like a magical place, but only he knew it was a place of sinners. He sat on a rock, a brooding shadow. He was the chosen one.
Not Joe
Lucky.

CHAPTER FORTY-FOUR

MAX
WAS HARVESTING
his final marijuana plants
when she came to him. . .pale and
beautiful, floating over the murmuring river.
Her slender arms held aloft a white burial robe.
Everything ceased singing on the earth and waters. Crickets and insects fell silent. Frogs leaped into the dark waters of the river. An owl stopped hooting.

A pair of Texas lovebirds in the willows took wing for Panocha Ridge, cooing off into the darkness.

La Llorona cried: "Donde estan mis hijos?"

The hair on Max's neck stood up. The color drained from his face. His legs quivered and became weak. He leaned against his truck so that he would not fall. He felt the urge for a bowel movement. Carefully, he removed the pistol from his pocket and placed it on the earth as a gesture of good will. He sank to his knees.

"Maria," he said, "spare this sinner. I'll fix my heart. I will leave my mota behind forever. This I promise."

She floated toward him, weeping in a sorrowful sound. She passed through him like a cold knife. His heart beat like a hummingbird's wings in his heaving chest. She turned and circled him.

La Llorona gave the most pitiful cry: a wail that traversed the ages. The agony of all women wronged by devious men. Max hoped he wouldn't have to pay for some pendejo's whoring transgression against her. Silently, he recited The Lord's Prayer.

He gazed into her beautiful face. Her black hair was wet from the water and hanging in limp strands. Her reds lips were inviting for a witch. And then he decided there was nothing to do but die. So he sobbed almost as profoundly as La Llorona. Then

she drifted up and over Max. She
passed like a mist through the
willows, but he could still
hear her wails. Max
stood up. And he
noticed he had
pissed his
pants.

CHAPTER FORTY-FIVE

FROM
OUT OF THE
night, the man dressed
in black walked along Highway
160 and appeared at the entrance gate
to the J. Lucky Ranch. His face was gaunt
and his body was as thin as a river reed. He
looked very much like the half-starved hermit. Even
his nose was thin, and the blue membranes were visible on the
surface. He lips were pinched like a man in misery. His eyes looked deranged and bloodshot. He carried a sign which proclaimed in fluorescent white:

"SINNERS REPENT!"

"Hear me ye sinners!" he shouted, "repent now, while the hour is upon us! The four horsemen will ride in vengeance! Repent!"

The Zoots and others exited RV's and campers and tents. Tiny Tim, his feet protruding out of his small tent, wiggled out and joined the Zoots.

"Repent your ass out of here!" Jimmy yelled at him.

"You shall tend the charcoal fires in hell, sinner!" the man in black shouted at Jimmy.

"You fool!" Claire said. "We're chosen ones."

"Chosen to guard the gates of hell for Satan!" replied the man in black.

Tiny Tim grabbed the sign and smashed it into pieces. A chorus of jeers and cheers rained down on the man in black. Silently, he picked up the pieces of his sign and walked back into the darkness from where he emerged.

"What the hell was that creepy thing?" Jimmy asked.

"A watermelon seed spat out by the devil," said Claire.

Inside the barn Joe Lucky poured milk into a bowl of Fruit

Loops. Alien creatures gleefully romped in a pool of water at the barn's pump. One alien popped out of the flying saucer and held Summer's blue-eyed doll. The supreme alien with the silver headband looked down at Joe Lucky from high on the barn wall and then leaped through space and landed in front of him. The alien dipped one finger into the cereal bowl and put the finger in its mouth.

"What's your name?" Joe Lucky asked. The supreme alien lovingly felt his face with long slender fingers. The creature droned in pleasure. It was at that moment that Joe Lucky knew he was right. These creatures were good. They held no malcontent or threat to humanity. They had just lost their way.
"I think you're a lady," Joe Lucky said. "I shall call you Gracie!"
Gracie leaped back up
into the rafters and
dangled there
like a
bat.

CHAPTER FORTY-SIX

SUMMER
SAT ON THE
sofa, reading from a
child's comic book version
of 'The Diary of Anne Frank.' "Mommy,
why did they want to kill Anne Frank?" Rachel
stirred pasta sauce in the kitchen. "People went mad in those days, honey."

"But she was just a little girl, like me."

"Yes, I know."

"Mommy, come in here and read this," Summer said.

Rachel wiped her hands on her apron and went into the living room. She sat next to Summer on the sofa, and looked into the book.

Rachel read, "How wonderful it is that nobody need wait a single moment before starting to improve the world."

She put the book down. "Honey, Anne Frank was a special little girl. So are you."

"Is that what daddy wants to do?"

Rachel felt water come into her eyes. "Your daddy thinks he can improve the world. But your daddy has too many thoughts in his head and sometimes those thoughts get tangled up."

"I miss daddy," Summer said.

"I know, honey. I need to finish that spaghetti sauce before Grandpa gets home." Rachel returned to the kitchen.

Summer sulked.

She clicked on the television with the remote. An attractive female news reporter announced:

"And in other news, a campaign is underway to help a Colorado man save his ranch. Children from all over the country are cashing in their piggy banks to help Joe Lucky, who is, by unconfirmed reports, harboring a UFO in his barn."

Rachel popped back into the room. She sat on the sofa.

The television news broadcast cut to children standing in

line at a bank and holding piggy banks of all sizes. Then it cut to two little girls selling lemonade from a stand. A banner was tacked onto the stand that proclaimed:

"HELP SAVE JOE LUCKY'S RANCH."

Automobiles on the street passed slowly and honked horns for moral support.

The news anchor said, "the government denies any UFO crash. But UFO sightings have increased worldwide. A farmer in Peru is said to have found a UFO. And the John Deere company has expressed interest in paying off the ranch note and truant taxes for Joe Lucky."

The television broadcast cut to the facade of a John Deere store.

"A spokesman for the tractor company said that the ranchers and farmers of America have made John Deere a resounding success. And perhaps, it's time for the company to give something back," said the news anchor.

"My Lord," uttered Rachel. She picked up the phone and called Joe Lucky.

But he was on his knees in front of the dog house.

"Come on, boy," he said, "you need to romp around." He filled Duke's bowl with Purina Chow. He didn't hear the telephone ringing inside the house. He did hear a swishing sound, like a rusty ceiling fan. Joe Lucky rose to his feet and looked up into the sky. He saw a black speck, and then the speck morphed into the shape of a helicopter.

Joe Lucky ran to the barn for his thirty-ought-six. The helicopter landed in his meadow. A man approached Joe Lucky. He was dapper in his suit and distinguished with his crop of white hair.

"Joe Lucky?" he asked.

"I'm Joe Lucky."

"Greetings from the President," he said, "I'm Will Chance, the Deputy Secretary of State. The President asked me to personally give you this letter."

He handed a letter to Joe Lucky.

"The President implores you, sir, to surrender the UFO for the security of the people and the country."

"I can't do that," said Joe Lucky, sadly.

"Why not?"

"Tell him sir, that if I do that, somebody would kill those beings in the name of science and technology."

"I ask you to reconsider."

"I have reconsidered a hundred times," said Joe Lucky. "I can sure use a million bucks, believe me. I have nothing left, sir, but my honor and my character. And character is not born onto a man. Character is hammered out by things like this."

"That's very eloquent, Mr. Lucky. You know this is dangerous business, son. There are darker elements that we cannot control. They want that UFO."

"I know."

Chance nodded and walked toward the helicopter, but turned and said, "do you have any final message for your President, son?"

"Yes I do," said Joe Lucky.

"Tell him, finders keepers, losers weepers."

The chopper floated into the dying light and passed as a shadow over the camp. The camp was in full-mode alert as people sat by the fence and peered up into the approaching darkness with their telescopes. The Zoots were having a peaceful moment on top of the RV. Jimmy smoked a joint.

Tiny Tim was a solitary figure at the gate, gazing off into the dying red embers on the horizon. A sleek silver limousine exited Highway 160 and darted through the entrance gate for the ranch, nearly running over Tiny Tim.

In Joe Lucky's yard, expensive Italian loafers swung out of the limo and plopped down into the dust. Flashy Gordon sported a pin-striped suit. His hair was slicked back as neat as a seal, and his narrow face hinted of a shyster. He waved for his chauffeur to honk the horn. Flashy leaned on the tractor parked in front of the barn doors. Joe Lucky came through the small swinging door of the barn and crawled under the tractor. He whacked dust from his jeans.

"I presume you are the famous Joe Lucky?" said Flashy.

"That's right."

"I'm Flashy Gordon and the best damn agent on the planet. I represent some famous people, including the quarterback for the New York Jets."

"I haven't played football since high school," said Joe Lucky.

"You're a true American hero, Joe. I don't know if you have a flying saucer or not. I really don't care. But I think you and I could sell more Hanes than Michael Jordan!"

"I don't wear Hanes," Joe Lucky said.

"No matter. We can do the whole market! We can sell everything from Cheerios to Viagra! Can you see it? From children, your biggest fans, to impotence. The whole enchilada, my friend. You're the new rave, son." Flashy pulled out a contract and pen. "Just put your John Henry right here."

Joe Lucky looked at the contract and ripped it in half. He deposited the pieces in Flashy's suit pocket.

"My father never gave me anything but a good lickin'. He told me once to stand firm and take your lickin', and he told me to be true to your word, your work and your friends. I took that advice to heart. No deal, Mr. Flashy."

Flashy Gordon kicked at a tire and then boarded the limo.

Turning down money, thought Joe Lucky, was hard to do.

Even for Miss Julie One Owl.

"We're in the fields of clover," she sang happily. Mayor Salazar and Julie One Owl watched laborers refurbish the vacant building next door to her cafe.

"I'm glad to see you broaden your horizons," said Salazar.

Hammers rang in the hot sun. Two laborers hoisted up a new sign:

"JULIE'S TORTILLA FACTORY."

"It's too bad the bishop of Pueblo doesn't agree with us,"

lamented Salazar.

"Yes, I know," replied Julie One Owl.

Down the street, a procession exited the church and marched toward the cafe. Padre Gomez toted the Holy Tortilla in the glass case. Citizens carried the statue of the Virgin de Guadalupe on top of a platform. She was adorned with beautiful wild flowers and gold and red silk. The procession sang an old Spanish song praising the generosity of the Virgin for the crops in the fields. Tourists on both sides of the street enjoyed the spectacle. Cameras clicked. Mariachi trumpets and guitars broke out into an endearing song. Pachuco brought up the rear. His chickens pecked along behind him. When all attention was on the tortilla factory, Pachuco removed a piece of loose plaster from behind the head of the Virgin and retrieved his Spanish bota made of goatskin. It was the perfect hiding place for his vino, he had thought. Padre Gomez frowned on his Mescal drinking, at least while he was in the shadow of the church. But the bota had a leak. He squeezed the bota and red wine spurted out. Aiiiiii, he thought, my wine is the source of the miracle tears! He merged himself into the crowd to make an escape back to his truck.

Father Gomez presented the Holy Tortilla to Julie One Owl.

"By order of the most Holy Bishop," said Padre Gomez, "the Holy Tortilla must be removed from the church. Sadly, it is not deemed a holy icon."

The procession booed.

Padre Gomez sprinkled Holy Water on the glass box, onto Carlota's mural, and finally into the entrance of the new tortilla factory.

The procession cheered. Hats sailed up in the air.

Padre Gomez said to Julie One Owl: "It must go back to the place where it was conceived. Or close enough, next door."

Mayor Salazar stepped forth.

"Neighbors! I'm overjoyed to announce that Julie One Owl has signed a contract with Wal-Mart and other prominent outlets to distribute her brand of tortillas. This new venture will bring jobs and more prosperity to San Miguel!"

The procession cheered louder. Next door, Max lay on the bed inside his repair shop. A stall was used as his sleeping quarters and office. Photographs of naked women were tacked onto the walls. Used tires were in racks on the wall. There was an old Ford Mustang up on jacks and the hood was open to display only disconnected wires. Greasy tools were everywhere. Max looked pale and sick.

The haunting down on the Conjeos had greatly altered his frame of mind.

He could hear the joyous celebration next door. He didn't
 care. When he closed his eyes, all he could see was
  the face of La Llorna, and he wondered how
   many children she had drowned in the
    rivers and lakes? She had spared
     him for a reason. But when
      he went bathroom in
       his pants, well, it
        was a dishonor
         worse than
          death.

CHAPTER FORTY-SEVEN

THE
BARN GLOWED
in the moonlight. Duke
emerged from the dog house
and looked at the orange light pulsating
through the cracks on the barn. He ate a few Purina
Chow nuggets, lapped up some water and went back into his abode. Inside the barn, Joe Lucky was sleeping on his cot. The creatures were inside the flying saucer and sleeping in their own alien dreams.

Down the road, the UFO camp was put to bed. The man in black sat against the pole of the entrance gate with his sign between his legs. There were no sinners to agitate and so he drifted off to sleep. Across the highway, the Billy Batty Show was quiet and still in the night. The ferris wheel reposed in the sky. The carousal horses were frozen in mid-gallop. The freak show was locked down.

Sheriff Ortega pulled up to Billy Batty's trailer and knocked on the door. Billy Batty opened the door wearing purple silk pajamas.

"Good evening," said Ortega.

"Hello Sheriff," answered Billy Batty.

"May I come inside?"

Billy Batty moved aside. Ortega entered and looked around the messy quarters. Empty gin bottles were everywhere. Stale pizza and half-eaten hamburgers were piled on the tiny table. There was also a stack of money.

"How is business?" asked Ortega.

"Well," said Billy Batty, "I'm not making enough to purchase a roller coaster ride." He put the stack of bills into a tin can, and then put the tin can into a battered old safe.

"I have to shut you down," said Ortega.

"What for?"

"You need a permit to have a carnival."

"How much is a permit?" Billy Batty spun the combination lock on the safe.

"Three hundred dollars. It's city law."

"You people don't change!" exclaimed Billy Batty, red-faced. "You still wait for some hapless fellow to come down the road. You're nothing but banditos!"

General Snoopy Taylor yelled into the phone.

"Listen you idiot, you need to take some drastic measures."

The whole world was displayed on blue monitors inside NORAD. Specialists manned the screens of bleeps and buzzes. Captain Jack walked the floor and looked into a monitor with the famous boot of Italy on the screen, and wondered if the Pope was caught up in the Joe Lucky mess?

Banker Goff sat rigidly at his desk in Alama and listened to Snoopy Taylor rant and rave on the phone. He explained to the general that John Deere paid off Joe Lucky's taxes and note.

"He owns the ranch," said Goff. "We're getting deposits in his name every hour. Joe Lucky is a wealthy man."

Snoopy kicked a trash can across the room.

"You're in it, mister!" Snoopy shouted into the phone.

"You're standing in the same shit pile as us!"

Goff hung up the phone. He walked through the bank lobby and went out the door.

Armed guards unloaded sacks of coins from a Wells-Fargo truck. They pushed the sacks into the bank on a dolly.

Goff removed his bifocals and polished the lens.

One guard stopped and asked, "can you get me Joe's autograph for my daughter? She told me not to come home without it." "Joe Lucky is the luckiest bastard in the world," Goff muttered.

CHAPTER FORTY-EIGHT

A
FIGURE
dressed in black
fatigues slipped through
the night and passed like a
shadow inside Joe Lucky's house.
Cowboy boots squeaked like mice across
the living room floor and into the bedroom.
Moonlight poured through the bedroom window. The figure removed a pistol with a silencer and placed the barrel on the shape of the head. He hesitated and listened to something thumping off in the night...thump...thump..thump.

And then he pulled the trigger twice, rapid fire, pouf...pouf. He pulled back the sheet and saw the styrofoam head with two smoking black holes. CIA Bill clubbed the head into styrofoam mush with his pistol. Then he heard the sound of a Black Hawk helicopter, a distinct sound of terror and death. He turned and saw a missile coming straight for the bedroom window.

"Well, piss in my boots!" he said.

CIA Bill saw a bright orange flash of light and then he was hurled into eternity.

The helicopter zipped over the burning ball of a house and faded into the night. A smoking boot landed in front of the dog house. Duke shot out like a spitball and fetched the smoking boot in his mouth. He ran off into the meadow. Whimpering, Duke scratched a hole in the earth and dropped the boot into the hole. He reversed himself, and used his back legs to frantically cover the boot.

Joe Lucky crawled through the swinging door and propelled himself from under the tractor. He ran to the house. The Porky Pig wind chime on the porch jingled from the heat of the fire. Joe Lucky sank to his knees.

Ortega and Billy Batty had heard the explosion and

exited the trailer. They noticed the ball of fire in the distance. Ortega ran for his truck.

"What the hell was that?" asked Billy Batty.

"Maybe another UFO crashed," said Ortega, "it's getting to be a regular UFO parking lot around here."

Duke ran to Joe Lucky and lay down by his side. He licked Joe Lucky's hand. The whole roof of the house dropped down in a crash of flames and smoke.

Ortega's Dodge Ram roared up to Joe Lucky. He leaped out of his truck and approached.

"I'm sorry, Joe," he said. "This thing has got out of hand."

Joe Lucky sobbed. "I lost everything, Ortega. My wife. My daughter. My ranch. My house."

Ortega sat on the ground beside Joe Lucky. He offered Joe Lucky a stick of Juicy Fruit gum. Joe Lucky refused.

"Not your ranch, pendejo."

Joe Lucky looked at him.

"What?"

"You don't know? Of course not, living in the barn like the horse you are. John Deere paid your notes and taxes. Children and charity people have been sending money to your bank account. Some rich bastard is going to match the final tally from the kids. God knows who else."

"Why?" Joe asked mystified.

"By now, you're the richest cabron in the valley."

Ortega chomped on his gum. They watched the flames consume the house. Only the porch stood upright and the Porky Pig chime jingled merrily away. "You're a bigger hero than Pancho Villa," said Ortega. "Everyone's in the clover. Julie One Owl signed a contract to publish a comic book about the valley. She just opened a tortilla factory. And that pinche Max Campos is selling weed by the ton. San Miguel is a big hit like Disneyland. And you, amigo, happen to be Donald Duck."

CHAPTER FORTY-NINE

A
NEW ONE
came knocking at
the barn doors. Harvey
Fields was prissy. He wore black-
rimmed glasses and loud colors to suggest
he was on the other side of the fence. When Joe
Lucky moved his tractor and invited him into the barn,
he put his palm to his mouth. "Oh, dear me," he exclaimed
in a shrill voice, "they are just lovely!" He patted Joe Lucky on
the shoulder. "I simply adore them. Mr. Lucky I think we can do something with your work."

"Did you see the flying saucer?" Joe asked, perplexed.

"Oh, darling, the only interest I have in space is when a piece of art fills it," Harvey said.

He walked around the barn looking up in admiration at Joe Lucky's sculptures. He fetched a shovel and twirled a sculpture. "You are the Henry Moore of welding. Look at that piece! It's just like Henry's 'Man Enters The Cosmos!' I saw that piece in Chicago." He noticed Snippy. He put his fist under his hairless chin. "If you autograph the horse, I could sell that too," he said.

"Snippy? He's only worth seven bucks on eBay," said Joe Lucky.

"That was moons ago," mused Harvey. "Your name is famous now."

"Are you saying that you can sell my art just because of my name?" asked Joe Lucky, disappointed.

"Well, we might have to bend a rod or two," said Harvey, "give a little more control to the compositions. But nothing drastic, dear. I can put your work in the best art galleries in New York and Paris."

"I never sold a piece," confessed Joe Lucky.

"Dear man," said Harvey, "I never met an artist who could sell anything. That is why you need a manager like me. I'll send a truck for all of them."

He clapped his hands. "Deal?" Joe Lucky pondered. "What do you think each one is worth?" he asked. "Oh, how you artist's fret so much, my lord," said Harvey.

"Artists are full of ego. I would say $100,000 to $150,000, give or take." Joe Lucky turned down a lot of things in his life. But he couldn't, no matter how his conscience pricked at him, turn down the chance to become an artist. Hell, he would cut his ear off, too, if that's what it took. "Deal," said Joe Lucky.

CHAPTER FIFTY

BILLY
BATTY ACCELERATED
his automobile down Highway
160. In the distance he saw something
on the road. He hit the brakes and swerved to
miss a man dressed in black who was standing on the center lane of the highway, holding a sign. He honked the horn at the imbecile. Man, Billy Batty thought, God forgot to pass our some brains for this patch of isolated earth.

Billy Batty pulled up at the mayor's office and stormed into the tiny building. Mayor Salazar was behind his desk smoking a cigar.

"What kind of racket you got here, Mr. Mayor?" asked Billy Batty.

"Racket? We don't have any Mafia in the valley. We have some Italians but they are just farmers." He blew a perfect smoke ring at Billy Batty. "I don't think the mob sees any money in potatoes."

"I need a god damn permit," Billy Batty said. He counted out three hundred dollars.

"Mucho gracias." Salazar scooped up the bills and deposited the money into a desk drawer. The drawer was full of neatly wrapped bills.

"Shouldn't that go to the County Treasurer?" asked Billy Batty.

"I'm the Treasurer and the Assessor. And if you find a wonderful little chica in San Miguel, I can marry you, too, as Justice Of The Peace."

Billy Batty roared back down Highway 160, feeling that he just got his pockets picked. He was sorry he had pulled his traveling show into San Miguel. They greased him like a squeaky wheel. They were greater crooks than him, and that hurt his feelings.

Next to his carnival, three teepees had sprung up on the

earth, and glowed iridescent from lanterns and hot flashes of intense light. The teepee skins looked beautiful with the artwork of racing ponies and grazing buffalo. He pondered this new development. Maybe he could hire them as a new attraction. Everybody loved an Indian show. At any rate, they couldn't hurt his business unless they sold snow cones. He approached the teepees and could hear the guttural and mysterious songs from inside.

He lingered at the flap of a teepee.

"Stranger, come forth," said an old voice.

Billy Batty entered the teepee and saw an old Indian sitting near a fire. The heavy smoke curled upward and exited through a hole in the teepee. The old man shook ceremonial rattles made from translucent skins. They were filled with clear quartz crystals. The friction produced flashes of bright light. He wore a beaded headband and leather vest. He had a pony tail of long grey hair, and his face was as wrinkled and brown as Mother Earth.

The old man shook his rattle at Billy Batty and used an eagle feather to fan smoke from a bundle of sage burning on a flat rock.

"Join me," he said.

Billy Batty sat Indian style. The Indian smelled really old, like smoke from a hundred camp fires.

"I am praying for the lights," said the old man.

"What lights?" asked Billy Batty.

"The fire rainbow," said the old man. "It will appear soon."

"Who are you?" asked Billy Batty. He could hear chanting from the other teepees.

"I am a Ute," answered the old man. "We lived here for many winters. We are the people of the shining mountains. It was time for me to return." He shook his rattle in flashes of light.

"Chew this," he said, and reached into a vest and gave Billy Batty a round wad. It smelled bitter.

Billy Batty tossed it in his mouth and chewed the sour button, and promptly went on the roller coaster ride of his life.

Time passed.

But he didn't know exactly how much. An hour? A day? A week? He listened to ancient songs. He watched the old Indian do the Spring Bear Dance, as his legs pounded in rhythmic motion on the ground. His shadow danced on the teepee hide.

And then a coyote wandered into the teepee and sat on his haunches next to Billy Batty. The Indian huddled back down at the fire. The coyote looked directly into Billy Batty's eyes. The coyote panted, tongue protruding out of its mouth.

"The trickster sees the coyote in you, white man," said the old Ute. "Let him tell you a story:"

"Once upon a time, a long time ago, Coyote and his wife lived near a happy Ute village. A great ceremony was planned in two days. There would be dancing and eating and much singing for the ceremony. The women would bake bread and prepare buffalo meat to get ready.

But nobody had any salt.

Now, Mrs. Coyote said to her husband, go get a bag of salt from the Salt Lake. I will stay home and bake the bread and prepare the meat. So, Mr. Coyote ran off to the Salt Lake. When he arrived, he was very tired from the journey. So he thought he could get some sleep before he filled the bag of salt.

A magpie landed on him. He thought of a trick he could play on Coyote. He went and got more magpies. They all lifted sleeping Coyote and carried him back to his lodge and put him back in his buffalo robe. When Coyote awoke, he thought he had been dreaming when his wife said he had to go to Salt Lake to get salt for the buffalo meat. His wife entered the lodge. Coyote knew it was not a dream. She said, why are you so lazy and can't do a chore of fetching some salt? She poured a water bucket on his head.

He went back to Salt Lake the next day. When he got there, the same thing happened. And the next day he ran back to the Salt Lake for the third time, and filled his bag of salt. Then he fell down again into a deep slumber. This time the magpies took pity on him and took him back to his lodge with the bag of salt.

And the people rejoiced as Mrs. Coyote got to salt the buffalo meat."

Billy Batty smiled. The coyote licked his face while he was prone on the ground. He was no longer inside the teepee. The old man stood over him and fanned sage smoke down on him. And he saw butterflies floating all around. He looked up into the sky.

Billy Batty saw the rare fire rainbow.

A wondrous phenomenon when cirrus clouds with just the right amount of ice crystals are hit precisely by fifty eight degrees of the sun.

It was as if God put orange and yellow paint onto his palette and brushed strokes of flames onto the blue sky. And the flames curled upward, as if caught by wind, and reached its flaming fingers into the very steep heavens.

Billy Batty discovered a bag on his chest. He sat up and dipped his finger into the bag and tasted salt. Coyote had left him the bag of salt as a sign. He rose to his feet and saw the man in black toting his sign and trotting up the highway.

Claire was broiling steaks on the grill when the man in black took up his relentless pacing at the gate. The campers had launched a twilight baseball game in Joe Lucky's meadow.

"Repent! The rapture is now," shouted the man in black. "He's coming because men are lovers of themselves, lovers of money, boasters, blasphemers, unholy, unloving, unforgiving, slanderers, brutal, despisers of good, traitors, lovers of the dark rather than the light, lovers of pleasure rather than God."

"Boy," declared Jimmy, "the man has a GE electric motor in his mouth."

Tiny Tim looked at the man in black with disdain.

Across the highway, the carnival was back in business. There was a line at the pay booth. People tossed darts at balloons for stuffed animal prizes. There were shrieks from inside the snakeman show. Children threw tantrums for cotton candy. The merry-go-round and ferris wheel spun to bad music and joyful cheers.

And Billy Batty sat in front of his trailer.

He had been blessed as a trickster. That was a great honor for a thief like him.

Peace finally came to the valley.

The sun was setting in a bloody ball on top of the Sangre de Cristo Mountains. Meadow larks flew low to the earth, wings dipping down to touch the blades of grass. The Texas doves cooed from Panocha Ridge. The windmill twirled on its weary plight to suck water out of Joe Lucky's meadow. The fire rainbow had passed away and left the sky streaked with purple bruises.

Joe Lucky sat on his tractor and breathed in the smell of sage. He puttered off for his mail.

At the gate, a crowd had gathered to greet Joe Lucky. He leaped off the tractor. "Good evening," he said to the crowd.

"Hello, Joe," said voices.

Jimmy approached. "Sorry about your ranch, Joe," he said.

Joe Lucky nodded.

Quick as a blink, the man in black ran forth, shouting:

"Joe Lucky is the anti-christ! You're the spawn of the devil! Go to hell with your father!"

He pulled a pistol and fired point blank at Joe Lucky.

Everyone but Joe Lucky struggled to breathe.

Joe Lucky looked down at a hole in his shirt. A tiny wisp of smoke came swirling out of the hole. His face displayed utter surprise. Slowly, he sank to his knees.

"He shot the blessed one!" said Claire, her clenched fists to her mouth. The crowd moved slowly forward. Joe Lucky toppled into the dust. With one glassy eye, Joe Lucky could see the beauty of the bloody sunset.

Only then did he know how much he wanted to live. How much he wanted to kiss Rachel. And hug Summer just one more time.

The crowd turned on the man in black with a vengeance of flying fists and boots and curses.

Jimmy ordered: "Take Joe to the RV! Hurry!"

Two men picked up Joe Lucky and rushed him into the RV. Tiny Tim turned his attention to the man in black moaning on the ground. He picked up the man in black by the neck and carried him off to his Jetta.

Jimmy and Claire sped off with Joe Lucky gasping for air in the rear of the RV. Claire wiped his brow with a damp cloth.

"Oh God!" Claire uttered.

"Hang in there, Joe," said Jimmy.

The RV passed the Jetta on Highway 160. Ortega raced in the opposite direction with red lights flashing.

Tiny Tim held the pistol like a toy in his big hand. The man in black was slumped in the passenger's seat.

"You heathen," he shouted at Tiny Tim. "Where you taking me?"

"To jail," said Tiny Tim.

"You freak! Let me go, you freaky freak!"

"Shut up!" said Tiny Tim.

The man in black reached across and struck Tiny Tim in the cheek with his balled fist. Tiny Tim never flinched.

Tiny Tim saw the alligator farm sign. On impulse, he turned the steering wheel and exited for the alligator farm. The man in black was convulsing and frothing at the mouth. "Devil," he managed to exclaim.

Tiny Tim pulled up to a large pond, surrounded by chain link fence. Lights on poles illuminated the pond. In the distance, dogs barked from the farm house. Tiny Tim hauled the man in black out of the Jetta and carried him to the entrance gate of the pond. The man in black kicked and squirmed in his grasp.

"Let me go, you child of the devil!"

Tiny Tim unlocked the gate and quickly pitched the man in black into the pond like a horseshoe toss. The man in black thrashed in the murky water. There was a crunching sound.

"Repent!" said the man in black. He went under water. He bobbed up. "Sinner," he said. Tiny Tim saw a flash of teeth. The man in black went under again with a gurgling sound. He bobbed up to say: "Oh dear, this hurts." There was another crunching sound and the man in black disappeared. Tiny Tim watched for another bob. There was none. He stood there and watched one last bubble rise to the surface and pop into oblivion.

The bullet, an inch from his Joe Lucky's heart, was surgically removed at the Alama Hospital. The doctor, himself sweating bullets, had lifted up Joe's beating heart and removed the thirty-eight slug.

"Look at this," he said to the surgical team, "you can measure the human heart by grams, and yet it can hold all the joy and sorrow of the world."

Everyone looked down at Joe Lucky's bright, red, beating heart. Then he was wheeled to intensive care and hooked up to machines and IV's. Needles were stuck into both of his arms. His face was pale and puffy.

In a waiting room, Padre Gomez, Sheriff Ortega, Julie One Owl, Dino, Ducky, Mayor Salazar, Jimmy, Claire, Max, Tiny Tim and a sprinkling of UFO nuts paced nervously into each other.

"It's all a plot to kill Joe," Julie One Owl said.

"Las hierbas malas no se mueren," said Max.

"What the hell does that mean?" asked Jimmy.

"Bad herbs don't die," translated Julie One Owl. "Shut up Max. We got problems here. They'll take the UFO. We have to stop them."

"In regards to the law," said Ortega, "the shooter has disappeared. If Joe dies, I want this shooter for murder. Anyone know where he's at?"

"The government probably scooped him up," said Max. "He's probably getting the water board torture right now."

"Well," said Jimmy, "it couldn't happen to a nicer guy."

"This UFO conflict is also a matter of business," said Mayor Salazar. "We lose that UFO, we lose our tourists. We need some muscle. We need to call the vatos and low riders."

"Yeah, that would give them somebody else to shoot instead of each other," said Max.

Julie One Owl poured a cup of coffee into a styrofoam cup. "We have a lot of mystic stuff here in the valley. I think we're in the center of the earth. When I was a student at Adams State, I did a paper on Juan Baptiste de Anza."

"Who's he?" Max asked.

"He was the Territorial Governor of New Mexico," Julie One Owl explained. "In his diary of 1777 he describes strange lights flying around our mountain."

"So," said Dino, "I see them every night."

"I'm just saying that this UFO chose this place," said Julie One Owl. "I think we live in the middle of a super space highway."

"Yeah," scoffed Max, "Interstate UFO 90. Speed limit 5,000,000 miles an hour. Go get the speeders, Ortega."

Julie One Owl looked at Max with anger. "Juan Baptiste de Anza also wrote of a powerful low humming sound coming from the mountain."

"They claim there's an underground UFO base in our mountains," said Ducky. "It has to be alien if he saw and heard that."

"Why does it have to be alien?" Dino inquired.

"You sure ain't the brightest lightbulb in the gym," said Ducky. "George Washington had the first set of false teeth in America, but I don't think he had a secret UFO base in 1777."

Claire piped in, "I think it's a religious cult like Jim Jones. And that man in black was the reverend."

"That could be," suggested Dino. "Cults and aliens both sacrifice animals, including our cows and horses."

"Cayete tu voca," said Max. "You rustle more cows than the flying saucers cut up!"

Dino shrugged sheepishly.

Rachel and Summer rushed into the hospital. They had motored from Denver to the valley in just five hours. They ran for the waiting room, both frightened and pale.

"How is Joe? What happened?" asked Rachel.

"He was shot," said Julie One Owl.

"Thanks for letting us know Sheriff Ortega," said Rachel. "I knew something like this would happen."

"The nurse told us the bullet did a U-turn in front of his heart, nicked a rib, and bounced behind the heart," said Jimmy. "A true miracle. We've been waiting a few hours for more information. I think God spared him. We should pray for Joe."

They formed into a circle. Padre Gomez recited the "Lord's Prayer", and everyone prayed.

Rachel and Summer rushed off to see Joe Lucky. In Intensive Care, they pulled up chairs at his bedside. They held his hands.

"Joe, honey, please forgive me," said Rachel, leaning down to kiss him on the head.

"Me, too, daddy," said Summer. She stroked his limp hand. "You can call me happy feet. You can call me Summer and the fish. I don't care."

Joe Lucky's eyes fluttered at the sound of Summer's voice. "I hope you found your goodness, daddy?" "Yes, Mr. Joe," said Rachel. "Now, I believe Anne Frank." She smiled at Summer. "And, in spite of everything, we still believe that people are good at heart." "Daddy, did you hear mommy?" "He heard me, honey."

CHAPTER FIFTY-ONE

ON
HIGHWAY
160, a long line of low
riders came glistening in
the sun. They roared through the
gate and formed a colorful skirmish line
across Joe Lucky's dirt road. Much to the cheers
of the camp, they bounced their shiny grills up and down
like speed boats crashing on waves. The low riders debarked
wearing leather vests and bandannas on their heads. They had
guns galore. Some wore belts of bullets around their chests,
like revolutionists. Again, the camp cheered their funk
and spunk. Tiny Tim had tinkered with the gears of
the tractor until he could go forward and in
reverse. He bounced down the road towards
the ranch; then, reversing the tractor
next to the barn doors, he took up
stewardship of the charred house
and barn. He sat, emotionless,
in the hot sun, and listened
to the Porky Pig chime
tingle from the
blackened
porch.

CHAPTER FIFTY-TWO

JOE
LUCKY
dreamed he was
on Panocha Ridge. He
could see his ranch and it
was full of morning light and promise.
He could see Summer and Rachel down at
the windmill and he could hear their happy voices
carry and float up to him. He could hear Duke barking
excitedly. The sun was shining and the Texas doves were cooing in the cool recesses of the cliff. And he could see the Conejos River as if God tossed down a silver ribbon from the heavens and it curled up on the green earth. And he could see the Sangre de Cristo Mountains and the San Juan Mountains, old and familiar guardians of the ancient valley.

All this he could see and he was happy.

A black hawk hunted in the sky, like a smudge of soot.

And he leaped off the ridge and floated with the hawk over his ranch, over the Conejos River, over the tiny town of San Miguel, and in his exaltation of flight he knew how much he loved this valley.

He knew he could never leave it. Not even for a million dollars. His grandfather, grandmother, mother and father rested under identical white, wooden crosses in the San Miguel graveyard. He was bonded by his ancestors' bones to the land.

In his flight, he saw Tiny Tim sitting diligently on his tractor in front of the barn. He had a guardian. He could see LRRP's watching Tiny Tim from the meadow, crawling like snakes in the grass. Occasionally, a laser light from a rifle danced on Tiny Tim's massive chest. And then he saw Rachel and Summer arrive in the Ford Bronco. They walked to the house and looked at the destruction.

Rachel sighed, "oh my Lord."

Tiny Tim stepped off the tractor and approached them.

"Are you Bigfoot?" asked Summer, holding her I-pod fish.

"No, but I got big feet," answered Tiny Tim. He stomped his feet into the dust. "See. Hello, I'm Tiny Tim. I'm guarding the barn."

"Who burned our house, Tim?" asked Rachel.

"Some say the Army dropped a bomb," said Tim. "Others say it was a gas leak."

Summer went to the doghouse and peered inside. "Duke?"

"He's in the barn," explained Tiny Tim. "He took up with the aliens."

They walked toward the barn. Summer called for the dog. Duke emerged from the swinging door and shot out from under the tractor. He leaped up into Summer's arms, licking her face and almost knocking her to the ground.

"I haven't seen them yet," said Tiny Tim, "but I hear them sometimes."

"Are they still in the barn?" asked Rachel.

"Yes, they are. Joe put the tractor in front of the doors to protect them. He cut out a swinging door. I'm too big for the swinging door so I stay on the tractor."

"How long you been here, Tiny?" Rachel asked.

"Since they shot Joe."

"Oh, you poor man," she said. "Summer and I can watch the barn. Go on home, Tiny."

Tiny Tim reached up and retrieved the rifle from the tractor. He handed it to Rachel. The giant walked off down the dirt road.

"Mommy?" said Summer.

"It's alright, honey. They didn't hurt daddy so I don't think they will hurt us."

"I know. Daddy said they were good."

She crawled under the tractor pushing the rifle ahead of her. Summer followed through the swinging door. They looked at the slick and silver UFO. Duke came through the door wagging his tail and rendered a half-hearted bark at the UFO.

"I just think they want to go home," explained Rachel.

"Are we going to sleep in here?"

"Yes, honey. Just until daddy is better."

"Where are they?" asked Summer.

"Probably taking a nap inside the ship," explained Rachel.

Rachel walked over to the sleeping quarters. She leaned the rifle against a rafter, and fixed the blanket on the cot. She went to the table.

"Look, honey, daddy brought Fruit Loops."

Outside, Drone planes glided across a full moon.

The UFO camp was on heightened alert and everyone was on guard and looking into their telescopes. They had taken the precaution of planting armed guards around the perimeter of the camp. Hopeful voices rose everywhere from the camp as mischievous lights arced and soared across the starry heavens. A million moths fluttered around the lanterns on the tables. Jimmy and Claire sat outside the RV, lounging in their lawn chairs. Jimmy slapped at annoying mosquitoes.

Tiny Tim stood at the fence and gazed off into the distance.

"Damn bugs are worse than Vietnam," complained Jimmy.

"You never went to Vietnam," corrected Claire.

"Well, that's one reason why I didn't go," explained Jimmy.

"I wonder what goes on in Tiny Tim's head?" asked Claire.

"Who knows," said Jimmy. "But he's a nice fellow."

"Yes, he is," Claire said. "But he is as strange as Joe Lucky."

Down at the barn, Summer's voice came out of the darkness.

"Itsy Bitsy Spider ran up the water sprout..."

Rachel was sleeping soundly on the cot.

"...down came the rain and washed the spider out."

Rachel shot up in bed, eyes wide.

"Summer?" she called. She picked up a flashlight and searched the dark nooks for her daughter.

"Summer? Where are you?"

Rachel bumped into the bony legs of Snippy and nearly died of fright. She could hear Summer's voice singing in the darkness, her voice as light as fluff in the air. Her flashlight beam searched frantically. She found Summer sitting on the ground, surrounded by aliens. They crouched in front of Summer. The big, blue-eyed doll sat against the barn wall.

"My God!" shrieked Rachel. Despite herself, Rachel felt

herself lose control. "Get away from her!" she shouted.

"No mommy! Don't scare them!"

Gracie reached for Summer, a maternal gesture; laying three fingers and palms on each side of her small face as if trying to reach for her thoughts. Summer looked into Gracie's big black eyes with wonder. Gracie turned, looked at Rachel, and droned. The aliens shot up to the roof and walls as if yanked by strings. Gracie scrambled off and squatted with palms on the sides of her silver band. She seemed to be transmitting thoughts from her mind, Rachel thought. She approached Gracie. Joe said your name is Gracie?" Gracie emitted a drone.

CHAPTER FIFTY-THREE

JOE
LUCKY
ran past beautiful
bronze sculptures, firmly
set into the earth, depicting The
Passion of the Christ. He followed
a twisting, rock-lined path leading to the
top of a hill. From the path, he could see the town and
the whole valley below. Fields of potatoes ran parallel to the mountains, and fields of alfalfa swayed in the breeze. The apple orchard was full of fruit and he could almost hear the fruitfall thumping on the earth. He ran frantically from one Station of the Cross to the next until he stumbled onto level ground. He knew he was at the sacred shrine on top of Calvary Hill. A bone-white shrine reposed in the twilight. It was mission-style with twin oval towers on the facade. The shrine was enclosed by a stone wall and small garden coves for prayer and reflection. And then he saw his beautiful creatures perched on the stone wall. They droned to each other. Gracie leaped down from one tower to look directly into his eyes. He sat on the wall and felt a great peace come into his heart.

Joe Lucky opened his eyes. A nurse was checking his pulse in a hospital room. "Welcome back, Joe Lucky," she said with a smile. "I need to go," Joe Lucky said, trying to rise in bed. "Where?" "I have to do something," he said.

"Yes you do. You have to rest," the nurse said.
"What happened?" asked Joe Lucky. "You
were shot. That bullet had some
sort of radar. It missed every
vital organ in your
body. Talk 'bout
some spin on
the cue
ball."

CHAPTER FIFTY-FOUR

SARAH
ORTEGA HAD
a baby bump in her
belly. And this provoked
Sheriff Ortega to author a shotgun
wedding. She stood before Padre Gomez in
her grandmother's white wedding dress carried
all the way from Taos, New Mexico nearly a century
ago. She held a bouquet of daisies. Jerry was decked
out in a bolo tie, white shirt and black pants. The night on
Panocha Ridge had inspired the emergency. They recited the
wedding vows and then the church bell rang joyously. Jerry
and Sarah ran out of the church and made a mad dash
through a rain of rice for Jerry's Chevy truck where
their DNA had merged months ago. Tin cans
were fastened to the rear bumper. As
they drove off, the cans banged on
the road. Dogs darted after the
truck, barking the length of
tiny San Miguel. And
all was good in
the Mexican
hamlet.

CHAPTER FIFTY-FIVE

JOE
LUCKY
recovered slowly.
After a week in Intensive
Care, he was moved to a hospital
room and took painful walks with Summer
in the hallway. After the third week he graduated
to a wheel chair and was strong enough to make his escape attempt by week four. Tiny Tim pushed him down the corridor and right out of the hospital. Joe Lucky basked in the freedom and warmth of the sun.

"It's a beautiful day," Joe Lucky said. "Now get me out of here before they summon Sheriff Ortega."

Tiny Tim picked up Joe Lucky like a child in his big arms and ran to the Jetta. He placed Joe Lucky in the passenger's seat, tossed in his bag of pain killers and made a clean escape. Joe Lucky rejoiced in the smells of the valley: the wheat fields and the pungent potato fields. He sucked the smell of sage into his lungs as they hurled down Highway 160.

They passed through the entrance gate to the shout of cheers. Inside the barn, Duke lifted his huge snout and dashed through the swinging door. He ran recklessly for the approaching Jetta. Joe Lucky rolled down his window.

"Hey there, Duke!" he said.

Duke overran the Jetta. He turned and followed in a cloud of dust. Summer and Rachel had crawled out of the barn and watched the Jetta come down the dirt road. They shouted in glee.

Joe Lucky exited slowly from the Jetta. "How are my girls?" he asked.

"Hello, honey," said Rachel. "Welcome home."

"What home?" Joe Lucky joked.

"We'll build a new one," Rachel said. She embraced Joe Lucky and planted a moist kiss on his lips. Summer hugged his unsteady legs.

"How are Gracie and my UFO friends?" asked Joe Lucky.

"They are charming guests," said Rachel.

Joe Lucky shook Tiny Tim's hand. "Thanks for everything, my big friend."

Tiny Tim smiled, and left in the Jetta.

Inside the barn, Gracie leaped down from the rafters to visit with Joe Lucky on the cot. She watched Rachel smear antibiotics onto the bullet hole with twenty stitches just below his left nipple. Tenderly, Rachel wrapped gauze around Joe Lucky's chest.

She had lost all apprehension of the aliens. Gracie laid one long slender finger on the gauze, trying to read Joe Lucky's hurt. Joe Lucky felt Gracie suck the pain out of his chest.

"Isn't she beautiful, honey?"

"Should I be jealous here?" Rachel asked.

Joe Lucky smiled. "I'm glad you came back."

"Me too."

Gracie looked at Rachel as if she understood their tenderness. Gracie leaped to the water pump and cupped water into her palm and licked water.

"I couldn't give them up," explained Joe Lucky. "No, you can't Joe," said Rachel. "I know where they want to go," said Joe Lucky. "I think Gracie sent a dream to me."

"Where?" asked Rachel. "Our shrine on the hill," he said. Duke curled up beneath Snippy. Summer played jacks on the ground as the other aliens curiously observed. They droned as she picked up each jack. Joe Lucky had his family back again.

CHAPTER FIFTY-SIX

SUMMER
WANTED TO
take her alien friends
to the swim tank. She insisted,
despite Joe Lucky's warning, that there
were some bad guys in the bushes. Duke chased
the aliens around the barn, barking as they zipped through the air like fanciful birds. Rachel and Gracie had bonded. She presented Gracie with a jade necklace. Gracie wore the jade around her translucent neck and fondled it with her three fingers.

"How did you make the doll come alive?" she asked Gracie.

Gracie just blinked her big black eyes. The aliens watched Summer labor on her coloring book, droning proudly of her accomplishments. They liked Joe Lucky's sculptures, and perched on them as watchful as eagles.

"Gracie has a crush on you," Rachel told Joe Lucky.

"I don't even know if she's a girl," confessed Joe Lucky.

"I think she's male and female," Rachel said.

"Can't tell," Joe Lucky said. "They are as transparent as glass. I think that is why they don't go out in the day. The sun would blister them to death."

The banker Goff had drove out to the ranch and presented Joe Lucky with two bags of money. Joe Lucky was waiting for the right time to show Rachel.

"Come look at this honey," he said, leading her to a dark corner where he lifted open a plank on the wall and pulled out the money bags. He scooped up a handful of bills and tossed them into the air.

"We're in the money," he sang.

"Joe, where did this come from?" exclaimed Rachel.

"From people I don't know," Joe Lucky said. "See my art work. You always hated them?"

"I don't hate them, Joe," she defended herself. "I just thought you would never sell them. Actually I think they're cute."

"Well, I sold them to a fellow from New York," said Joe Lucky. "He is going to sell them in his shop for three hundred grand for the whole lot. Maybe more."

"You're kidding me?"

"No, my love, I'm not." He tossed more bills into the air.

The commotion attracted Summer and the aliens. Summer ran to see what happened. The aliens scooted through the air in an attempt to catch the bills. Summer jumped up and collected one.

"Daddy, are we rich?" she asked.

"You bet," said Joe Lucky. "We're the richest family on earth." He kissed his wife and tossed more bills.

"Now that we're rich, daddy, can we take them to the swim tank?"

Joe Lucky looked at Rachel.

Rachel shrugged.

"What the hell," Joe Lucky said, "why do we have to hide in the barn? We're the good guys."

Rachel hoisted Summer onto the tractor and Joe Lucky cranked the motor. Timidly, the aliens came out of the barn and zipped through the evening's golden light. Gracie leaped from the barn's roof to the dog house to somewhere in the grassy meadow. The others followed, droning.

They bounced for the distant windmill, screaming like bungee jumpers.

Duke came like a gray bullet from the barn and circled the tank in a frenzy of barking.

"Seems our Duke has his second wind," said Joe Lucky.

"He's just happy, daddy," Summer explained.

"I'm happy, too. Last one in the tank is a fish!" he said.

They jumped into the tank with their clothes. Summer splashed. Joe Lucky and Rachel took up their spot by the water pipe.

"Look at them, Joe," she said. "They're beautiful creatures."

The aliens roosted on the windmill as white as plumb birds. Some leaped down to skim the water in the tank, and then taking flight again.

"Yes, they are. So are you."

"What are we going to do now, Joe?"

"Build a house. Take a honeymoon trip before Summer has to go to school."

"No, I mean about them." She pointed upward. "I know where
to take them," Joe said. Gracie hung from an iron beam and
stuck her three fingers into the gushing water from
the pipe. She licked her fingers. She droned in
joy as Summer paddled around like a beaver.
The moon peeped over Panocha Ridge. The
sky was flushed with the last golden
rays of day. The crickets began
to chirp in the meadow. And
from the cliffs of Panocha
Ridge, the Texas
doves cooed
incessant
songs of
love.

CHAPTER FIFTY-SEVEN

JOE
LUCKY
crashed through
the barn doors with the
UFO secured by cable to the four-
wheel trailer. Rachel rode in front of
him in the tractor. Summer sat on the gear box,
tiny arms clinging to Joe Lucky's legs. Duke sprinted
by the tractor and made a daredevil leap into Joe Lucky's lap. Joe Lucky propped Duke on the front of the tractor like a hood ornament. Duke sat on his haunches and watched the LRRP's pop out of their holes and approach menacingly through the tall grass of the meadow. They aimed red laser lights at the bouncing Lucky family. As the LRRP patrol approached, they triggered Joe Lucky's booby traps. Fireworks sailed up into the sky and blossomed into colorful flowers.

The UFO gleamed brilliantly in the fading sunlight. Its oval silver shape seemed to quiver in anticipation on the trailer. The lowriders leaped into their automobiles and opened a passageway. At the entrance gate, the Luckys were met with riotous cheers and the whole camp surged forward to greet this strange, beautiful vision. Joe stopped long enough for the people to leap onto the trailer and feel the UFO. They screamed in delight.

Jimmy and Claire and Tiny Tim walked forth in awe.

"Oh Jimmy, it's beautiful," said Claire, wiping at her eyes.

"It's the prettiest thing I ever gazed upon!" said Jimmy. He whacked Tiny Tim on his waist. "Look, Tiny!"

Shouting children gushed forth. They jumped like kangaroos in their excitement. The low riders roared in front of the tractor and took the point on Highway 160. The LRRP's advanced on the left side of the highway, ducking into the sagebrush, training lasers on Joe Lucky. The Zoots ran to their RV and took off so quickly that they ran over their own lawn chairs.

Tiny Tim followed in his Jetta, and the whole camp jammed into their vehicles and fell into a chaotic long line of bumper-to-bumper traffic. A hundred horns honked. Citizens from San Miguel came down the other side of the highway and turned abruptly to follow the procession. Julie One Owl, Dino, Max, Ducky, Padre Gomez, waving his bible, all hollered from the back of a pickup truck.

"Lordy, look at it!" said Ducky. "No wonder the pendejo didn't want anybody to get it!"

"Where's he going?" asked Max.

"Who knows?" said Julie One Owl, "just follow him."

Some citizens had rifles and pistols and they pumped them into the air to encourage Joe Lucky. On the tractor, Rachel planted a long kiss on Joe Lucky's lips.

"Joe, you're a hoot," she said.

"Are you getting excited, honey?" Joe Lucky asked.

"Not this time. I'm scared shitless," she answered.

"Me too," Joe Lucky said.

Captain Jack maneuvered the green Hummer along side of Joe Lucky's tractor. Above, helicopters gushed through the air ahead of the whole procession like black, angry hornets. Snoopy Taylor cursed the great exodus. He took up the radio phone.

"Nobody shoot a damn bullet!" he roared. "I want a no-fly zone for fifty miles. No press helicopters and no news vehicles."

A voice crackled over the radio: "General, what about the parade?"

"Let them pass," said Snoopy Taylor. "Just keep the press out. We can refute the rest of this debacle."

Some of the nuts passed the Hummer, irate at its slow pace. The Zoot RV kissed the Hummer's rear bumper.

"Ok, Claire, crank up the volume on Old Blue Eyes!"

Claire slipped a Frank Sinatra CD into the player.

"Fly Me To The Moon" crooned out of the speakers on top of the RV.

Ahead, Joe Lucky turned off Highway 160 and puttered up a hill. The whole comical procession followed. Max's truck pulled aside of Joe Lucky's tractor.

Rachel waved at him.

"I'd be proud to ride point for you, Joe," said Max, gunning his truck's motor. The truck farted out black smoke.

Joe smiled and gave him the 'thumbs up.' The pickup passed Joe Lucky and proceeded up the hill.

"I think we live in halves," said Joe Lucky, switching gears. The tractor groaned up the hill.

"Halves?" said Rachel.

"Yes, everything is in halves. Think about it. Mother-father. Sister-brother."

"Uncle-aunt," suggested Rachel. "Good-evil. Hope-despair."

"Love-hate," said Joe Lucky. "Night-day."

"Beauty and the beast," offered Summer.

"That's right, Happy Feet!" Joe exclaimed "What else? Sunrise-sunset."

"Funny-sad," said Rachel. "You're right Joe. We could go on forever."

"So what is the half of you, daddy," asked Summer.

"I'm glad you asked," he said tenderly, "your mommy is the half of me. And you're the half of us."

They bounced to the top of the hill. Joe Lucky puttered to a stop near the beautiful mission-style shrine, gleaming bone-white in the evening's light. Joe Lucky leaped off and helped Summer and Rachel to the ground.

"Joe, why can't I go up there with you?" Rachel asked.

"I don't know what will happen," he explained. He kissed her, "I never done this before."

"Joe Lucky," she said, "nobody has done this before."

He leaped back onto the tractor and reversed the UFO into the shrine courtyard. The shrine's twin towers penetrated the dark sky. The oval shapes on top of the shrine glistened like cat-eye marbles.

"I love you, Joe Lucky!" Rachel shouted.

The Hummer spearheaded a long line of headlights. The lights were a mile long. It took twenty minutes for the whole procession to reach the parking lot. Captain Jack and Snoopy Taylor stepped out of the Hummer.

"What the hell is he doing?" Snoopy Taylor asked.

Max stepped forth, "he's waiting."

"Who's this scamp, Jack? Stay Back!" ordered Snoopy Taylor.

"I'm not one of your Army cabrones!" said Max. "You're not the boss of me, jackass."

Everyone watched as Joe unfastened the cables around the UFO. The flying saucer seemed to sense its freedom and started to glow orange and red. The crowd uttered a loud and collective sigh.

Rachel, Tiny Tim and Summer walked in front of all the gawkers.

"Let them go home, daddy," said Summer.

"He is, honey. Your daddy has found the goodness."

Rachel started to cry.

They stood, hand-in-hand.

On the other side of the hill, LRRP's ran up the winding path and past the Stations of the Cross. They peered through night-vision goggles. The bronze sculptures of the Rapture appeared to glisten like gold in the moonlight. The LRRP's zigzagged higher up the path to reach the stone wall. They reposed their M-16's on the top of the wall and red lasers danced on the chest of Joe Lucky.

Sgt Reemes was at the wall. He said, "Stand down!"

On the left side of the shrine, the towering bronze Crucifixion of Christ stood gloriously against the dark sky. On the right side, beyond the simple courtyard, Christ stood on the cross, His body bent like a bow, and He lifted one arm up to heaven in supplication. He was eternally frozen in His final ascent to His Father.

Joe Lucky sat patiently on the tractor seat ignoring the laser lights on his body.

Below, Sheriff Ortega raced up the hill in his truck with red lights flashing He jumped out of his truck and saw citizens of San Miguel armed to the teeth.

"Put your guns away!" he ordered. "This is a place of peace and prayer!"

"We don't trust the Army," said Dino.

"We're Air Force!" explained Snoopy Taylor.

"Hell, Ortega," said Max, "we'll shoot this puto General just for his sassiness!"

"Sheriff Ortega is right," said Padre Gomez. "This is a place of peace."

Citizens tossed their weapons into the back of trucks.

Up in the heavens lightning bolts ripped through the sky. Most of the bystanders fell to their knees. Some dangled rosaries and muttered prayers.

And then the top of the UFO blinked open to release a powerful beam straight up into the turmoil in the turquoise sky. The aliens came out, moving in ecstasy, and leaping through space to cling onto the oval dome of the shrine. The bystanders cheered gleefully from the parking lot.

They hugged. They kissed. They danced and rejoiced in this wondrous sight.

Then, out of the crowd, a beautiful woman in a white dress launched into the song of "Ave Maria." Her graceful voice and haunting lyrics soared beyond the crowd and into the heart of Joe Lucky. Gracie emerged from the flying saucer and leaped across the courtyard to the cross of the Ascension. The song seemed to inspire her. Joe Lucky ran for the Ascension where Gracie hung from the cross. With one hand, Gracie lovingly touched the face of Jesus. She blinked her big black eyes at Joe Lucky. He smiled and sat down at the base of the station.

"Ave Maria" reached a higher and haunting power. Gracie leaned out from the cross and arced her head to listen.

More lightning flashed across the dark sky. Clouds opened magically to expose a thousand bright spinning lights. An alien leaped down to the wall and looked directly into the frightened eyes of a LRRP. The alien touched his M-16, and blinked at him. The others emerged and zipped through the night.

"Something's happening," said Julie One Owl, looking up into the sky.

The mother ship appeared out of the clouds, so big it slowly filled the whole sky and revolved in a million blinking lights.

Joe Lucky walked back to his tractor, looking up in awe.

Now, the crowd cowered in fear. Others stood transfixed and speechless, mouths opened.

"Damn it, Jack," mumbled Snoopy Taylor, "look at the technology we're losing."

"Just maybe," said Jack, "we're not ready for it."

Captain Jack hung his head to mutter his own prayer.

Joe Lucky climbed onto his tractor and watched the LRRP's go to their knees. The aliens sailed through the air and landed on the UFO. They went down the hatch. Gracie leaped from the Ascension to the hood of the tractor. She droned into Joe Lucky's face, telling him something.

And then Gracie did a thing that stunned Joe Lucky. She made the Sign Of The Cross.

"Do you know God?" Joe Lucky asked her.

Gracie blinked her big black eyes. She touched Joe Lucky on the lips. And then she leaped onto the UFO and went down the hatch. The UFO closed like an eyelid and melted into a smooth seamless mass.

The immense mother ship issued a vortex of swirling lights and slowly sucked the UFO up into a gap in the underbelly. The gap melted into a smooth surface. The mother ship leaped a great distance into the heavens like a time machine, and then made another leap into infinity. The heavens closed. Joe Lucky was crying. He stood on the tractor seat and lifted open palms to the heavens. He was soaked in moonlight. He looked up into the starry heavens. Slowly the serene sky was shattered into a dazzling show of lights. They soared and arced across the dark heavens. "I believe there is good in the world," said Joe Lucky.

ACKNOWLEDGMENTS

THE
AUTHOR
would like to thank
the following individuals
for their contributions to this novel.
The wonderful artwork for the book cover
by Carol Blatnick Barros. The beautifully scripted
Introduction by Robert "Doc" Leonetti. Editors: Robin
Roderick and "Doc" Leonetti, fine writers of their own merits.
Also Shannon Marshall who was there from the beginning,
and Linda Espinoza and Nancy Toupal who read the proof
copy. Bill Lash, who helped rescue the book from despair
with his computer graces, and Ron & Tammy
Lagerman for their expertise. Contributors:
Connie Givigliano and Donna Leonetti,
great sisters, who helped in many
ways. And Rita Montoya who
helped keep the author
grounded with
late night
phone
calls.

Joe And the UFO
is currently available at:

www.sentrybooks.com

A Great West Publishing Company

Great West Publishing
51 East 42nd Street
New York, NY 10017

Made in the USA
Columbia, SC
19 June 2023